WHERE DREAMS COME TRUE

The Daily Cruise Letter/The Daily Cruise News

Jukeboxes, soda floats and saddle shoes.

If you think you've stepped into a time warp on *Alexandra's Dream*, you're right. This special cruise is a salute to the fifties. Our staff will be wearing vintage clothes and uniforms, and our onboard stores and restaurants will all have a fifties twist. We hope you packed your own poodle skirts and bobby socks, but if you forgot, our shipboard boutiques feature accessories to get you in the mood.

And remember the Hollywood stars of the 1950s? Gorgeous, glamorous and larger than life, they sang and danced across stage and screen. As a special treat, we have invited some of your favorite stars back for a one-time reunion on stage. Our assistant cruise director Liam Bates is choreographing an original show featuring such Hollywood greats as Frederick Miles and Lily Simmons. Besides the show, the stars will be available for autograph sessions and Q and A after screenings of their films.

So even if you missed the fifties the first time around, you'll find that fun-packed decade yours to experience aboard *Alexandra's Dream*.

MICHELLE CELMER

lives in a southeastern Michigan zoo.

Well, okay, it's really a house, but with three teenagers, three dogs, three cats and a fifty-gallon tank full of a variety of marine life, sometimes it feels like a zoo. It's rarely quiet, seldom clean, and between after-school jobs, various extracurricular activities and band practice, getting everyone home at the same time to share a meal is next to impossible.

You can often find Michelle locked in her office writing her heart out and loving the fact that she doesn't have to leave the house to go to work, or even change out of her pajamas.

Michelle *loves* to hear from her readers. Drop her a line at P.O. Box 300, Clawson, MI 48017, or visit her Web site at www.michellecelmer.com.

Mediterranean NIGHTS™

Michelle Celmer

STARSTRUCK

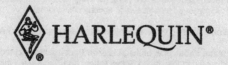

HARLEQUIN®

TORONTO • NEW YORK • LONDON
AMSTERDAM • PARIS • SYDNEY • HAMBURG
STOCKHOLM • ATHENS • TOKYO • MILAN • MADRID
PRAGUE • WARSAW • BUDAPEST • AUCKLAND

ISBN-13: 978-0-373-38970-4
ISBN-10: 0-373-38970-1

STARSTRUCK

Dear Reader,

As a writer there is nothing more fun than creating new characters and learning who they are—their backgrounds, likes and dislikes, personality quirks. To me they are living, breathing people, even if they exist only in my head and within the pages of my books. And as with everyone in my life, some are dearer to me than others.

That's how it is with Claire and Liam. I really *liked* them.

I didn't actually create Liam for this book. He has been living in my head for years, just hanging out, waiting for the right book to come along. But only as I delved into his background did I realize what a complex, compelling and appealing man he is. This is a guy who really has his head together. He knows exactly what he wants. At least, he thinks he does. Until he meets Claire.

Claire was a tough nut to crack. I tried to get in her head and she fought me tooth and nail. Every time I came close to figuring her out, she would throw up another roadblock. Only after I stopped pushing, let her set the pace, did she reveal herself to me. And thankfully Liam's subtle yet direct approach was just what she needed to break out of her shell.

While writing this book I found myself dealing with two people who couldn't be more different, or more perfect for each other. I hope you enjoy their journey as much as I did.

Regards,

Michelle Celmer

Writing can be a lonely business,
so it is a pure joy to have the opportunity to work
with so many talented and truly wonderful women.

Ingrid, Joanne, Cindy, Cindi, Carol,
Karen, Dorien, Diana, Mary, Sarah and Marcia,
it has been a pleasure.

DON'T MISS THE STORIES OF

Mediterranean NIGHTS™

PROLOGUE

WHO WOULD IT BE THIS TIME?

Tracy smoothed her poodle skirt and slapped on a plastic smile, watching with voracious eyes as the guests boarded the ship, wondering who would find the pendant. It might be several days before she figured it out. But she was getting desperate, the desire to see her son a tense knot of longing in her belly.

She'd screwed up the last time. She'd let herself become too attached. She wouldn't be making that mistake again.

That morning, she'd been watching Patti, had seen her open the safe and take the pendant out. The cruise director had run her fingers over the tarnished metal, as though it were precious, and not a hunk of cheap silver.

Only Tracy knew the truth. What lay hidden underneath.

When Patti had set out to hide the pendant for the cruise ship treasure hunt, Tracy's heart thudded in her chest, hands trembled with anticipation.

Keep it cool, she'd warned herself. Don't make her

suspicious. If she blew her cover, Tracy might never see her son again. "Who is the lucky passenger this time?" she had asked casually.

Patti had shrugged and slipped the pendant in her uniform pocket, a secretive smile curving her lips. "We shall see."

Tracy's fingers had itched to snatch it from her, but she couldn't be that obvious.

So she had followed Patti, determined to see in which stateroom she hid the pendant. Then she would simply wait until she was gone, go back and steal it, and leave this miserable ship and her job as a dancer forever.

And she would have succeeded this time if Liam, the assistant cruise director on *Alexandra's Dream,* hadn't stopped her to remind her that it was time to get into costume. Her back was turned for only a second or two, but when she looked, Patti was gone. Tracy had searched for her, panic twisting her insides, hoping to see her emerge from a cabin. But it was too late.

She clenched and unclenched her hands now, digging her nails into the flesh of her palms, watching the passengers file by. She smiled when necessary, said her cheerful, "welcomes," but on the inside she felt tied in knots. Her past failures marked her, oozed from her pores like a slowly spreading stain. The sour stench of her own fear filled her nose.

Salvatore was growing restless. There was no telling what he might do if she failed again. What if he decided he didn't need her any longer, but figured she knew too much? Then it wouldn't be only her son's life in danger.

Her little boy needed her. Meaning she had only one choice.

This time she *couldn't* fail.

CHAPTER ONE

CLAIRE MACKENZIE FELT as if she'd been transported back in time.

The female staff wore poodle skirts and sweaters with bobby socks and saddle shoes, or fitted pencil skirts, and blouses with what her grandmother used to call Peter Pan collars. Some of the men looked like greasers in their white T-shirts and jeans and ducktail hairstyles. Others appeared more Ivy League in plaid shirts, slacks and polished loafers.

The truth was, she'd felt a little weird dressing retro fifties to board *Alexandra's Dream,* but her grandfather had insisted. As a Hollywood star from the fifties, Frederick Miles had been invited on the themed cruise along with other former actors to celebrate their contribution to stage and screen. "I'm a guest," he'd told her. "We have to look the part."

To make him happy, since that's what this cruise was all about, she'd hit the vintage shops and ransacked Papaw's attic, where he still stored her grandma's dresses and gowns, all the while wondering if people were going to point and snicker. But much to her surprise, everyone, staff and guests alike, took this fifties theme business very seriously.

"So, what do you think?" he asked, a note of enthusiasm in his voice that lifted her heart.

"You were right, Papaw," she conceded. "We fit right in."

A gleam of excitement lit his eyes. One she hadn't seen for quite some time. Rarely since his stroke two years ago, when he had officially retired from acting. And certainly not since her grandmother passed last spring.

He was happy. And that made her happy, too. With all of the activities the ship had lined up for him, the interviews and autograph signings, the rehearsals and special luncheons, she had a feeling the next ten days would fly by.

She was almost able to stop worrying that the glitch in the irrigation system of her organic herb business back on Saltspring Island hadn't been fixed. Suppose René wasn't paying attention and the seedlings were overwatered? Or even worse, *under*-watered. The last time she took a few days off to visit her grandfather, two shipments of fresh organic herbs had been switched accidentally and it took an hour of major butt-kissing to keep from losing the distributors. She shuddered to imagine all that could go wrong in an entire week.

Ugh. When had she become so responsible? Ten years ago, she wouldn't have been able to hold down a steady job. She wouldn't have *wanted* to. Life had been one big party. Now her life revolved around running the nursery.

She itched to pick up her cell phone and make a quick call to one of her employees, but everyone had strict orders that if they saw her number on the caller I.D. to let it ring.

"You're going to have fun," René had insisted just before she left. "Just forget about work."

Easy for him to say. He had a wife and kids. He had a *life*. These days, work was all she had.

"You had better not be thinking about work," Papaw warned. Did he know her or what? "This is a vacation."

"I know. I'm doing my best."

"Our rooms are on the Artemis deck. We can take the elevator up."

She had expected the ship to have a closed-in, claustrophobic feel, but as they walked to the elevator, she was struck by the sheer size of the lobby. The high ceilings and sweeping architecture. The buffed and polished accents. The uncertainty that had been churning in her belly transformed to honest to goodness excitement.

Her mother, Mira, had originally planned to take the trip with Papaw. She had agreed—however grudgingly—that Papaw was getting too old to travel alone. But in usual Mira fashion, she had called with some sob story about feeling too fragile to travel.

Whatever *that* meant. Mira had been clean and sober for several years now, or so she claimed. So what possible reason could she have to feel fragile? This trip would have given her and Papaw a chance to spend some time together, an opportunity to reconnect and, with any luck, overcome a lifetime of adversity.

Leave it to Mira to let them all down.

Claire suspected that her mother had fallen off the wagon one too many times. And landed on her head. Or maybe she had been born screwed up. A few essential wires crossed or something. She had never been what a person would consider normal.

Of course, neither was most of the population of Hollywood, where Claire had been raised. She was third generation Tinsel Town Brat. Had she chosen to pursue acting, her family would have been right in line with the Barrymores. But Claire had seen too many of her friends ruin their lives in the Hollywood scene. She had broken free just in time.

They boarded the elevator with a family of four, a young couple with two adorable little girls dressed in matching poodle skirts and saddle shoes. The wife immediately recognized Claire's grandfather and nudged her spouse.

"That's Frederick Miles," Claire heard her whisper, and felt a familiar rush of pride. After all these years, he still turned heads.

"Could we get your autograph, Mr. Miles?" the husband asked, holding out the brochure with Papaw's picture on the front. "We're huge fans."

Her grandfather beamed. He still loved the attention, loved to be in the spotlight. "It would be a pleasure."

"This is *Frederick Miles,* the famous actor," the mom

told the little girls, as if she were introducing royalty. And even though they were probably too young to know Frederick Miles from Captain Crunch, they stared up at him in awe.

Claire stood inconspicuously at the back of the elevator, content to remain invisible. It was rare that people recognized her these days. A decade ago she was a household name. The Paris Hilton of the early nineties. Granted, her bank balance was several millions smaller, but she made up for that in wild, erratic behavior and scandal.

"They were friendly," Papaw said as they reached their deck and the elevator doors closed behind them.

"Of course they were. You're the star of the cruise."

He didn't say a word, but his smile spoke volumes—and stayed fixed in place until they reached their rooms. Despite his gregarious on-screen manner, her grandfather was often a man of few words. A thinker, who in his eighties still possessed a keen intellect and sharp wit.

It was his body that was having trouble keeping up.

She used the card key to unlock her door. "I'm going to freshen up, then we can go exploring."

He opened his own door. "Don't take too long, now."

She stepped into her room—a *premier* stateroom, she'd been told when they checked in—and sighed with appreciation. The first word that came to mind was opulent.

It was larger than she'd expected, not unlike a regular hotel room, and decorated in seashell-pink and mother-of-pearl. A billowy duvet covered the king size bed, piled high with satin pillows.

Just for fun, she flopped down on her back and felt her body sink into the creamy softness. Mira had no idea what she was missing.

An enormous welcome basket, wrapped in shimmering cellophane, sat on the table beside the love seat. She rolled off the bed to take a peek. Without breaking the seal, she could see that the items inside were gourmet treats that would do nothing for her waistline, all in what looked like authentic vintage packaging.

The cruise line was going all out for this fifties theme.

She walked over to what she assumed was a window and thrust the curtains aside, flooding the room with the pinkish-orange glow of sunset. And a breathtaking view from her own personal balcony. She slid open the door, and a rush of sea air rolled in to greet her. She breathed in its salty essence, felt the sharp edge of her nerves bevel. Only then did she appreciate just how badly she needed this.

Ten days to let loose. She winced. In the past when she *let loose*, the police had always ended up involved.

But not for a long time. She had learned to suppress that other part of her. The wild child. Maybe deep down she'd been worried that if she let go at all, once she got started, she wouldn't be able to stop.

She fished her makeup bag from her purse and stepped into the bathroom. It was decorated in the same downy hues as the bedroom, with gleaming gold fixtures and delicious tile.

She opened her case and fished her hairbrush out, tugging it through the long auburn hair that she'd inherited from her father. She'd gotten the freckles and fair skin from him, too, and the constant need for sunblock.

She washed her hands, but when she grabbed a towel from the rack, something slipped from inside it and landed with a loud clink on the tile floor.

What the—

She crouched down and reached behind the commode to pick it up. Cold metal draped over her fingers…a silver chain with a slightly tarnished pendant in the shape of a teardrop. It looked old and well-worn.

And…*cheap*.

How in the heck did it manage to get stuck in her towel? She would have to turn it in to security when she and Papaw went exploring.

She checked her reflection. Passable. The makeup could use a touch-up, but really, who did she have to impress?

She grabbed her purse, made sure she had her card key, and stepped into the hall. Her grandfather must have been eager to get going, because he opened the door seconds after she knocked.

"Ready to explore?" he asked eagerly.

"We have to make a quick stop at the front desk, or security." She showed him the necklace. "It was wedged between the towels in my bathroom. Someone must have left it there by accident."

He took it from her, turning it over in his hand to examine the tarnished silver. "Huh. I would think security would be the place to go."

She slipped the necklace into her purse. "To security it is."

AFTER A BIT OF SEARCHING, and a few stops to sign autographs and meet an adoring fan or two, they found the security office. The staff here appeared to be the only ones not participating in the themed costumes.

The officer behind the desk, an older, stern looking woman, gave Claire the distinct impression that she had seen the necklace before. Had it been reported lost? Or even stolen? She picked up the phone and talked quietly for a moment, her eyes on Claire. And Claire began to get the sinking sensation she had done something wrong, or was in some sort of trouble.

Her grandfather seemed to grow wary of the situation as well. "Maybe they think we stole it," he whispered.

Their concerns seemed founded when the woman hung up the phone, gestured to one of the security officers and said, "Would you please escort these guests to Ms. Kennedy's office."

"Who is Ms. Kennedy?" Claire asked.

She held the necklace out for Claire to take. "The cruise director."

Why did they have to see the cruise director? Why couldn't they just leave the necklace here? And if it was lost or stolen, why give it back to her?

"Have we done something wrong?" Papaw asked.

"Ms. Kennedy will explain."

They were ushered out the door, and though no one had been rude or outwardly threatening, Claire felt as though they were being asked to walk the plank.

Patti Kennedy, an attractive, dark-haired woman, dressed in a vintage airline stewardess uniform, met them at the door of her office and greeted them with a smile. "It's a pleasure to meet you both. I'm Patti Kennedy, the cruise director." She shook both their hands. "I hear you've found something interesting in your room."

Claire showed her the necklace. "It was caught inside the towel in my bathroom. Maybe it belongs to a member of your staff?"

"Actually," Patti said with a grin, "it belongs to you for this trip."

"To me?"

Patti laughed. "You'll find an explanation in the orientation material. If you open the folder, you'll see a colored glossy flyer with the heading 'Teardrops of the Moon.' It's a treasure hunt we've developed on board for fun. It's based on a legend about the moon goddess and her shepherd lover. When he was killed, one of her tears encased a diamond that she'd given him, and ever since, teardrop pendants have been a tradition, especially with Greek brides. We hide the necklace in a stateroom for one of our passengers to find. According to the legend, the necklace is supposed to bring good luck."

Claire looked at the bulky piece. This thing was lucky? "Really?"

Patti nodded, and with a gleam of what looked like mischief in her eyes, said, "Especially in love."

Now Claire *knew* it was just a legend. Not only did she not believe in good luck, she believed even less in love. A lesson she had learned the hard way.

"You look skeptical," Patti said.

"Claire is something of a pessimist when it comes to romance," her grandfather explained.

Claire nudged him with her elbow and said in a stern voice, *"Papaw."*

He shrugged. "It's true."

Not everyone could have the ideal relationship he and her grandma had had. Wedded bliss for almost fifty years. Some people just weren't capable.

"If you wear it, you'll also find that you get special treatment from the staff," Patti said.

"I'm just happy to know that it wasn't lost," Claire told her.

"Is there anything else I can do for you while you're here?"

"I think we're all set," Papaw told her. "Thank you for your help."

"If you have any other questions or concerns, please don't hesitate to ask. And enjoy your cruise."

Claire thanked the cruise director, and as they stepped out of her office, she slipped the necklace into her purse.

Papaw saw her do it, and the stern expression that she remembered so vividly from her childhood settled into his face. In a way it was a comfort. He seemed younger when he looked at her that way. Not that he was limping around with one foot in the grave. But despite months of physical therapy, the stroke had changed him, and losing her grandma had robbed him of that last hint of youth. "Aren't you going to wear it?"

She shrugged. "It's kind of…ugly."

His blatant disappointment filled her to the eyeballs with guilt. "Do it for me."

"Fine." She fished the pendant out of her purse and slipped it over her head. It felt cool against her skin. "Happy?"

"Very happy," he said with a smile, and she could see that he meant it. And for that, she was happy, too. When he turned away she discretely tucked it under the collar of her blouse. "Where to now?"

"How about a walk on the deck? I'll bet the stars are really something."

"Sounds good."

"Mr. Miles!" a man called in a refined and tidy British accent. The silky smooth tenor vibrated through her skin, plucking away at her nerve endings. A funny little quiver raised the hair on her arms and the nape of her neck.

Whoa. That was weird.

She was afraid to look. Afraid to spoil it. What if the face didn't match the voice? What if the guy was a toad? And what difference would it make?

If there was one thing Claire had grown used to over the years, it was men disappointing her.

CHAPTER TWO

THEY BOTH TURNED in the direction of the voice and Claire's first impression of the man sprinting toward them was the utter length of him. He was decked out in a vintage, casual navy uniform, every part of him long and lean. Slim, but solid.

He greeted her grandfather with a warm handshake—the two-handed kind. "I'm Liam Bates, the assistant cruise director. It's an honor to have you aboard, sir."

Automatically her eyes followed the length of his toned arms. Lean biceps, tanned forearms, all the way to his hands. Some women judged a man by his eyes, some preferred a cute butt, or whatever body part they found particularly appealing. For whatever reason, Claire had a thing for hands. Give her a decent pair of hands to work with and she could forgive an imperfection or two.

This man's, she realized immediately, were a work of art. Finely boned with long, tapered fingers. Not too harsh or veiny, or even worse, knobby. But not too feminine either. The sort she imagined might belong to an artist or musician. Hands that would know a woman's body, mold and shape it the way a sculptor manipulated clay.

Graceful hands.

Her gaze traveled upward until it collided with eyes a clear, shocking blue, as though he'd captured the ocean's essence in his irises.

This man was no toad.

His complexion was as fair as her own, and despite the fact that his short blond hair was showing the signs of thinning at the corners of his forehead, it did nothing to detract from a face that was as eloquent and compelling as the rest of him. She would go so far as to say he was pretty, but his features were too masculine to be considered anything but handsome.

When was the last time she'd looked at a man and hadn't thought, *never in a million years?*

"So pleased to meet you," Papaw said.

He pumped Papaw's hand enthusiastically. "Sir, I assure you, the pleasure is all mine. I'm a huge fan of your work."

In his usual, humble way, her grandfather waved off the compliment. "The way I hear it you've had quite a career yourself."

"Some film and theater, yes." He turned to Claire. His eyes locked on hers and held, and she got another one of those odd little shivery feelings. "Would this be your granddaughter?"

There was a look of recognition in his eyes, one that clearly said he knew exactly who she was.

"Claire Mackenzie," she said, hesitating an instant before taking the hand he extended. But the idea of touching him was too compelling to resist.

Long fingers, surprisingly smooth, warm skin gobbled up her hand. His grip was firm without being overbearing. Friendly but not suggestive. "It's nice to meet you, Mr. Bates."

"Please, call me Liam." He retained his grip on her hand a second longer, letting go at precisely the proper moment. The instant before a friendly handshake became a veiled proposition.

"If there's anything I can get for you, I'm only a phone call away." He was addressing them both, but his eyes were still on Claire.

"Claire and I were just about to head out exploring," Frederick said, and Claire couldn't help but wonder if that wasn't some sort of veiled invitation.

Liam finally pulled his eyes from her to address her grandfather. "Excellent. Then I won't keep you."

Was that a dash of disappointment she just felt? What was wrong with her? It must be the pendant, she decided. Not that she believed it was somehow mystically altering her brain waves, but the power of suggestion could be a dangerous thing.

"I just wanted to let you know that our first rehearsal for Friday's show is tomorrow at ten a.m. on deck six in the auditorium," Liam said. "We'll break for lunch at noon, then return at two for a final two hours."

"What sort of show will it be?" she asked Liam, and when he looked at her, it was as though he knew exactly what was going on inside her head. But how could he? She'd had years to perfect her poker face. Even if she did find the man incredibly appealing, she would never let it show.

"It's a tribute to actors and films of your grandfather's era. A Hollywood review, if you will. Singing, dancing. We have an exceptional cast, but your grandfather is of course the star. It will be quite fantastic."

She didn't doubt that it would be. "I can't wait."

With the ghost of a smile lurking in the depths of his eyes, he nodded. A slight tip of his head. "Enjoy your evening."

Claire had to force herself not to watch him walk away. Besides, she knew without even looking that he had a perfect butt to go along with the rest of his perfect features.

"Nice young fellow," Papaw said.

She smiled vaguely and uttered a noncommittal, "Hmmm."

His brow spiked with curiosity. "You don't think so?"

He knew exactly what she thought of Liam. Papaw might have been getting up there in years, but he didn't miss a thing. He knew Claire well enough to see past all the emotional barricades to her true feelings. The thought was as comforting as it was annoying. "He's swell," she said, in fifties lingo. "A real dreamboat."

"My agent had wonderful things to say about him," Papaw said. "A talented fellow. And *single*."

Oh no, he was not going to try to set her up. "How would your agent know that?"

"Did you see a wedding ring?"

"Unmarried does not equate with single. For all you know he could have a steady girlfriend, or for that matter a *boyfriend*."

He flashed her one of those exasperated looks.

"Besides, I'm sure the ship has some sort of regulation against passengers fraternizing with the staff."

"I remember a time when that would have made him irresistible."

Maybe, but Claire had learned a lot since then. "I didn't come on this trip to meet men. I came to be with you."

"In other words, butt out." He sighed deeply and shrugged. "You win. I'll back off. Now why don't we take that walk?"

That was a little too easy. As he took her arm and they walked to the door, she couldn't escape the feeling that she hadn't heard the last of this.

CALL IT A HUNCH, OR intuition, or a touch of the second sense his mum swore she possessed, but it had been clear to Liam, from the instant he laid eyes on Claire Mackenzie, that she would be trouble.

And yes, all those rumors he'd heard about her, the things he had read in tabloids and gossip rags, might have had something to do with it. Although, to be fair, he hadn't seen her name in print for several years now. After her last brush with the authorities she had dropped off the map.

He watched her as she flipped through a magazine

in the coffee shop while she waited for her latte. The fifties clothing suited her somehow. The conservative button-up blouse, sporty capri pants and baby-doll shoes. And the silk scarf she tied around her throat was a nice touch.

She used to be...*flashy*. A party girl. Now she looked a bit more average.

Average height and weight, average build. Fair skin, high cheekbones. And freckles, for which he'd always held a fondness. The long, silky reddish-brown hair that she used to wear gelled and spiked now hung long and straight, nearly to the middle of her back, and only the color made her stand out from every other guest.

That and her eyes. They were large and inquisitive and the most unique shade of green. Mold-green, his father the pragmatist would have called it. The soft, fuzzy sort he might have seen on a bit of spoiled cheese in the icebox.

If there had ever been any spoiled cheese in the icebox. In a family of nine, food went quickly. In fact, one had to be aggressive at the supper table for fear that he might otherwise starve to death. That left no room to be persnickety. In the Bates residence, you ate what was put in front of you, or you didn't eat at all.

Latte in hand, Claire turned and did a quick scan of the shop, looking for an empty table. When she noticed him sitting there, she blinked with surprise, much the way she had last night when they first met. There had been a connection. Something about her that was oddly familiar.

He gestured to the empty chair across from him and waved her over. She hesitated for several seconds, as though she were weighing her options. If he didn't know better, he might have thought she was afraid of him. But a woman like her wouldn't be afraid of anyone.

Finally she wove her way through the crowded tables to where he sat.

"Good morning, Ms. Mackenzie." He rose to his feet and pulled the empty chair out for her. "Would you care to join me?"

"I don't want to disturb you."

"It's not an imposition," he assured her. "The truth is, I was hoping to talk with you about your grandfather. Have a seat."

Somewhat reluctantly she set her coffee down, hung her purse on the back of the chair and sat.

He sat back down. "You're an early riser."

"Habit. I'm usually at work before seven."

He'd imagined her the stay-up-all-night-and-sleep-all-day type. "Where do you work?"

"I manage a nursery that grows organic herbs."

"In the States?"

She shook her head. "On the west coast of Canada. You had a question about my grandfather?"

So much for small talk. "I wanted to inquire about Mr. Miles's health. The show I have planned does require a certain amount of physical activity. I just want to be sure that he's up to the task."

"I take it you know about his stroke."

"I had heard something, yes." Frederick Miles's agent had assured Liam that he was in tip-top shape, but Liam wasn't taking any chances. "I know that this will be his first performance since then. His well-being is my number one priority."

"He's had extensive physical therapy. His doctor assures me that he's bounced back remarkably well considering his age."

There was a hesitation. Something she wasn't telling him. "But?"

She shrugged. "I'm overprotective. Papaw tells me I worry too much."

"You have my word that I won't push him too hard."

"This probably won't make much sense, but I would prefer you not give him special treatment. He wants to do this. He *needs* to do it, to feel…normal. That won't happen if he suspects you're coddling him."

So it would be a precarious balancing act. Well, the more challenging the better, as far as he was concerned. "If it would ease your mind, you're welcome to sit in on rehearsal."

She stared at him with assessing, slightly narrowed eyes, as though she was attempting to read his thoughts. To figure out if he was sincere.

"You know," he said. "I was wrong."

"Wrong about what?"

"Your eyes. They're not moldy at all."

She blinked in confusion. *"Moldy?"*

Brilliant, Liam, call the woman moldy. "Sorry. I only meant that at first they looked to be more of a mold-green. I realize now they're actually closer to the color of moss. Brighter, I think. A bit more yellow than blue."

For a moment she only stared. Silent. Then she said, "If that's a pick-up line, you need to work on your material."

He grinned. It would seem the Claire he'd read about was still lurking around inside there somewhere. "I didn't mean to offend. I just have this annoying habit of saying what's on my mind."

One brow, a shade darker than her hair, arched slightly higher than the other. "They're in the same family, you know."

"Your eyes?"

"Mold and moss. They're in the fungus family."

"I didn't realize that," he said. "I'm afraid I don't know much about plants."

"Fungi aren't plants. They're heterotrophs."

He nodded, even though he didn't have the slightest clue what she was talking about. "I didn't realize that."

"Do you know what a heterotroph is?" There was a playfulness to her tone, a hint of amusement in her eyes. She was calling his bluff.

He shrugged. "I haven't the foggiest."

"Unlike a plant, heterotrophs don't fix their own carbon through photosynthesis. They use carbon fixed by other organisms for metabolism." She paused for a second, then asked, "Do you know what that means?"

Not a clue, but he found her fascinating none the less. He shook his head.

"Fungi are thought to be more closely related to animals than to plants."

He folded his arms across his chest. "You're different than I expected."

She took a sip of her latte, eyes never leaving his face, and said bluntly, "I take that to mean you've heard things about me."

The woman was a puzzle. Awkward and demure one moment, sharp and direct the next.

"Here and there," he admitted.

"That girl doesn't exist anymore."

In his experience, people could change all they liked on the outside, but the inside part was much harder to renovate. Whoever she was, he found her absolutely fascinating.

He glanced at his watch, disappointed to see that he had to leave if he planned to get to work on time. He would very much like to continue this conversation. He liked Claire Mackenzie, and he had a sense the feeling was mutual. "On that note, I'm afraid I have to get to work."

He downed the last of his coffee and pulled himself to his feet, offering a hand for her to shake. And as she clasped it, the warmth of her hand curling around his own, he felt it again. That zap of awareness. The eerie feeling of familiarity.

And he could tell, by the way she hesitated a second before tugging her hand free, by the perplexed look in her eyes, that she felt it, too.

"It was a pleasure talking to you, Ms. Mackenzie."

"Call me Claire," she said. "And if you really don't mind, I think I will sit in on rehearsal."

"Once you get to know me, Claire, you'll find that I never say anything that I don't sincerely mean."

"Then I'll see you at ten."

He was looking forward to it.

As he walked to the door, he knew without looking that she was watching him, trying to figure him out. Leading him to the conclusion that she was just as curious about him as he was her.

Although, at this point, he couldn't decide if that was a good or a bad thing.

HOW MUCH THEY HAD all aged, Frederick Miles realized as he wandered through the auditorium, mingling with the rest of the cast. There were fourteen in total.

He and his wife Marie had kept in touch with one or two of them. A Christmas or Easter card. An occasional e-mail. Television appearances. But most of them, people he used to consider his closest friends, he hadn't seen in years.

This past year, since he'd lost Marie, he'd felt as though he was just biding his time until he joined her. But he knew she wouldn't want that. And for the first time since then, he felt as if he had some sort of purpose. He felt alive again.

He looked out across the auditorium, imagining the seats full and the lights dimmed. Not a day passed that he didn't miss performing. Television or movies, theaters large or small. It didn't make a difference to him. It had been his life. His true purpose.

He heard the silvery tone of Claire's laughter and turned to see her talking with Eleanore Grant, Frederick's costar on a television series back in the late seventies.

As far as he was concerned, his granddaughter needed this trip nearly as much as he did. She worried him. It was time she came out of hiding, time she started living again.

Even though she had been a handful growing up, and there were times when she had pushed him and Marie to the breaking point, he missed the way she used to be. Fun and spontaneous and full of life. She'd gone from one extreme to another. Turned in on herself.

Just like her mother.

He loved Mira. She was his only child. His baby girl. But he'd given up trying to help her years ago, for fear that she would drag him down with her. She was like a black hole. She sucked people in, stretching them to the limit and ripping them apart. Mira was never happy with what she had, yet she never seemed willing to work for something better.

And he was ashamed to admit that at least part of the blame was his and Marie's. They had spoiled Mira. She'd never learned the value of a dollar. She'd never grown to appreciate the pride that came from hard work and determination. But rather than learn to cope, to try to better herself, she'd chosen to escape into the oblivion of narcotics and alcohol.

Claire had started down the same destructive path as her mother, although her drug of choice was isolation.

He had tried to convince her to move back to the U.S., but she claimed to be happy up in Canada. She said it felt like home. He suspected what she meant was that it kept her a safe distance from her mother and Mira's complicated life.

"Skip Miles."

At the sound of the familiar voice, the nickname only one person had ever used, Frederick froze, and for an instant he could swear his heart ceased to beat.

It couldn't be.

He had entertained the idea, if only briefly, that she might be here, knowing all along that it would be unlikely. Her career in film had been compelling, but short-lived.

For a moment he wondered if he might have conjured her up from his memory. A hallucination. But she was there. He felt her standing behind him. That crackle of awareness he so keenly recalled. The one he'd felt fifty-eight years ago, the moment he'd first laid eyes on her.

Anticipation and longing and a dozen other discombobulated feelings settled thick and heavy on his chest, threatening to drag him down to his knees.

Steeling himself, he turned, hands trembling in the pockets of his slacks, heart pounding so heavy against the wall of his chest he wondered if she could see it bouncing around under his shirt. "Lily Gordon."

Had that cool, calm reply really come from him? Two years retired and his acting skills hadn't rusted a bit.

"It's Lily Simmons now. I went back to my maiden name years ago." A tentative smile quivered across her lips. "It's been a long time. I thought maybe you didn't remember me."

Didn't remember her? He only wished that were true. But he would have known her face anywhere.

What man forgot his first love?

It astounded him, the ability to go so many years and still see people as they once were. To retain that sense of familiarity. Maybe that was a gift of age. Or in this case, a curse. Either way, she was a woman he wished he could have forgotten.

She'd allowed herself to age naturally, with grace and dignity. Her hair was as white as his own, her face lined by the years. She had sworn a long time ago that, unlike her spoiled and pampered mother, she would never resort to plastic surgery and hair dye and the latest miracle cream to retain her youth.

But she had promised so many things back then. Things that never came to pass.

Regardless, Lily had always been tough. Principled to a fault, and unquestionably dedicated to her family. Even if that meant sacrificing what had mattered most to her. Those traits he had most admired had ultimately been his and Lily's undoing.

"You haven't changed a bit," she said, her voice soft and unsure, eyes on her feet.

Maybe he hadn't, but she had, he realized. The deeper he looked, the more he recognized there was

something distinctly different about her. She looked…
ill at ease. Unsure of herself.

Demure.

What had happened to the firecracker who had
strutted out onto the set of her first major motion picture
ready to take on the world? The girl who belted out the
song lyrics like Ethel Murman's close cousin.

A moment of tense silence followed. Neither seemed
to know what to say next. Or maybe, there was nothing
left to say.

At that moment Liam propelled himself onto the
stage, rescuing them from the awkward lack of conversation. He clapped his hands and called, "Is everyone
ready to begin?"

When Frederick turned back to see Lily's reaction,
she was gone.

He had no reason to feel guilty, but he did anyway.

CHAPTER THREE

SOMETHING WAS WRONG.

Claire wasn't sure who that woman was talking with Papaw, but the tension building between them hung thick and syrupy in the auditorium. Whoever she was, she was making him upset.

Or maybe it was the other way around.

Claire was half a second away from marching up to intervene when Liam clapped to get everyone's attention and the woman walked away.

Liam hoisted himself up on stage, a swift, graceful lift of his body, as though he were weightless. For a brief moment she felt mesmerized. By the way he moved, the way he spoke. She'd never really had a thing for accents. Growing up in Hollywood, she'd hear them all. But there was something about his voice, the patterns of his speech. Refined but not snooty.

As though he sensed her watching, he turned in her direction, caught her gaze.

She'd met too many men who had a preconceived notion about her. The ones who believed that because they had seen her name in the paper, her picture plastered in the gossip rags, they knew who she was.

For some reason Liam seemed to be different. Not that she was ever a brilliant judge of character. Most of her missteps over the years, her disastrous relationships, were no one's fault but her own. She and Mira were very different in that respect. Claire took responsibility for her actions while her mother conveniently blamed everyone else for her own bad judgment.

If she were anywhere but here, Claire would have looked away. But for some reason the unfamiliar surroundings made her feel…less accountable somehow. She daringly held his gaze, just to see if she was still capable.

He grinned. An easy, flirtatious smile.

Then he *winked* at her.

Her heart fluttered.

Actually *fluttered* in her chest, as though a colony of moths had invaded her arteries. When he finally looked away, she felt the tiniest bit breathless.

"Shall we get started?" Liam called, and the cast began to file up onto the stage. Claire took a seat in the auditorium a few rows back.

He divided the cast into two groups, taking Papaw's group—including the mystery woman—for himself and assigning the remaining actors to his assistant, Tracy.

Liam lead with an informal yet firm approach. The cast appeared drawn to his charm, his contagious enthusiasm.

And so, Claire hated to admit, was she.

As a child, she had been carted along to countless rehearsals with her grandparents, and sometimes even with

Mira on the very rare instances when she had regular work. And though Claire had never caught the acting bug herself, when she wasn't causing trouble on the set and making a general nuisance of herself, she had watched and listened. Soaked it all in like a sponge. She could recognize the traits of a good director.

Liam was good. He had a gift.

And, oh, could he move. He demonstrated the choreography with the effortless elegance of a young Fred Astaire, and the raw sex appeal of a blond Antonio Banderas. He belted out the lyrics in a clear, bold tenor. A voice worthy of Broadway.

What was equally impressive was that he had written and produced the show himself. The songs he'd chosen, dance moves he'd incorporated, captured the finest of the fifties film era. Before her eyes she watched the cast bloom and come to life with the energy and vigor of performers half their ages.

Except Papaw. He appeared off somehow. Distracted. His attention constantly wandered back to the mystery woman, the one Liam called Lily, with a look that hovered somewhere between regret and longing.

Who was she? Claire knew the names and work of every other cast member. They were the true stars of their era. Except that woman.

At one point, when Lily looked his way and caught Papaw staring, he swung around so fast he collided with another cast member and nearly knocked them both to the ground. As soon as rehearsal ended, she walked to the stage to meet him. She cringed inside as he hobbled down the stairs toward her, frustration and exhaustion weighing heavily on his sagging shoulders.

"Escort me to lunch?" she said with a cheerful smile.

"Oh, sweetheart, I would love to, but I need to rest a bit before the second half. Guess I'm not as limber as I thought."

She hated to see him so discouraged. "You looked great up there."

They walked side by side up the aisle. "That's sweet of you to say, honey, but we both know I was awful."

"You weren't awful. Just a little rusty."

He cracked a grin. "On the bright side, that pretty young dancer, Tracy, has offered to work with me."

He opened the door for her and they stepped out into the hall. She walked with him to the elevator.

"Give it a day or two. You'll hit your stride." She smiled. "I know it'll be a great show."

"That Liam, he really seems to know his stuff."

"He does," she agreed.

"Bright and energetic. And talented." He shot Claire a sideways glance. "Nice young man, too."

She pasted on a sweet smile. "If you find him so appealing, maybe you should ask him to dinner."

He gave her one of those semi-stern, wholly exasperated looks. "You know, it wouldn't kill you to let loose and have a bit of fun."

She appreciated that he wanted her to have fun, wanted her to be happy, but this wasn't the way to do it. "Kind of ironic you should have to say that, considering for the first two-thirds of my life, I was constantly being accused of having *too much* fun."

He hooked an arm through hers. "That's my Claire. A woman of extremes."

He was right about that. "A family tradition."

"One I wouldn't mind seeing end." He patted her arm. "Do you still have the pendant?"

She pulled it out from under the collar of her blouse. "As promised."

"Good." He seemed to believe that it really was good luck.

She knew he meant well, but as close as she was to her grandfather, there was so much about her that he didn't know. And speaking of that, there seemed to be things she didn't know about him either.

"That reminds me," she said. "Who was that woman you were talking to right before rehearsal started? I don't recognize her."

Every inch of his body tensed, and his reply came out clipped and defensive. "I spoke to several women before rehearsal."

Whoa. What's this? He knew exactly who she meant. Why was he playing dumb? "I think her name is Lily."

He shrugged and looked away. "Just someone I used to work with. A long time ago."

"Have I ever met her?"

He shook his head, swatted away the suggestion as though it were a pesky fly. "She was out of the business long before you were born. I'm not even sure why she's here."

There was more to this than he was admitting, but he obviously wasn't ready to talk about it. And she knew him. Once he clammed up, truth serum wouldn't break his silence. She had no choice but to let it drop. For now.

He could be stubborn, but so could she.

"Mr. Miles, could I get your autograph?" she heard from behind them. And though she had half a notion to say he was too tired right now, she knew that wasn't what he would want. Frederick Miles never refused an autograph.

He turned to the middle-aged couple with a friendly smile. One autograph turned into two, then several more people stepped up to him, until he was surrounded by a small crowd.

She'd asked him once if it annoyed him, always being hounded by the public. He'd said simply, "Without the fans, I wouldn't be where I am."

That didn't mean the attention wouldn't sometimes take its toll on him. By the time they made it to the elevator, he looked ready to drop.

"Would you like me to bring you back something to eat?" she asked.

He shook his head. "I'll pick up a snack after practice this afternoon."

He looked so defeated. This trip was supposed to make him happy. "Are you okay, Papaw?"

He smiled and pressed a kiss to her temple. "Fine, sweetheart. Just tired. I'll feel better after a nap."

She had the feeling his frustration somehow revolved around that woman. But why?

The elevator door opened and he stepped in. "Have a good lunch."

She stood there until the door closed, fingering the pendant. She rubbed her thumb across its cool, uneven surface. She wasn't quite sure why, but it was a comfort.

"Looks as though I wore him out," a familiar voice said from behind her.

Claire dropped the pendant under her blouse and turned. Liam was grinning, of course. He seemed to do that an awful lot. His hair was damp with perspiration and his cheeks flushed. He gripped either end of the small white towel that hung around his shoulders, accentuating the lean muscle in his arms.

Claire's heart did that fluttery thing again. Did Liam feel it, too? This keen awareness? Or was he just being polite? Treating her well because of Papaw's connection to the show?

"He's discouraged," she admitted, and hoped Liam wouldn't hold his poor performance this morning against him.

"He shouldn't be. I have no doubt he'll bounce back. I thought you should know that, since you look a bit discouraged as well."

Did she? She hoped Papaw hadn't picked up on that. She wanted him to believe she had the utmost confidence in him.

"You needn't worry. I'm sure he'll do just fine."

"Maybe I'll stop by rehearsal again this afternoon. If that's okay."

"Of course. I guess I'll see you then."

"I guess so."

He hesitated, and she was sure he was going to say something else. Then he smiled, nodded, and walked away.

And she watched him, just as she had earlier in the coffee shop, and during rehearsal. Something about him fascinated her. What was it about him that made her feel so…vulnerable?

As he rounded the corner he looked back. She would have averted her eyes, but it was too late. She'd been caught staring. To look away now would only make matters worse.

His smile was the last thing she saw as he disappeared from view. Only then did she realize she'd been holding her breath. She breathed in and out a few times, just to be sure that she still could. She couldn't seem to shake that nervous, fluttery feeling in her stomach.

Though she never passed up a good meal, especially a free one, and the scents reaching out to her from the dining room were tempting, she had no appetite to speak of.

Instead of going to lunch, she decided to take a walk outside instead. Fresh air was probably all she needed. She was an outdoor person by nature. Being cooped up inside did funny things to her head.

That was why she was feeling so out of sorts, she decided.

A whirl of warm, salty sea air wooshed through her

hair as she stepped outside. The sun felt hot on her face and sounds of laughter and activity danced around her.

This was more like it. How could a person not get caught up in the excitement and fun? It was contagious.

She walked along by herself, stopping occasionally to watch the water lap up against the ship. Listening to the children chatter over the hum of the engine.

It was like paradise.

Then she saw a man dive into the pool. He was tall and slim with short blond hair. And though she only saw him from behind, he looked a lot like Liam. Like before, her heart started bouncing around her chest and her head had a strange, almost surreal feeling.

She stood watching as the man sliced through the water and emerged at the opposite end. And when he turned her way, a rush of disappointment slammed her from every direction.

It wasn't him. Although this man was similarly built, she could see now that he was younger than Liam and not nearly as attractive. He lacked that special…*something*.

Uh-oh.

Suddenly she understood what was going on here. It had been so long since she'd had these feelings, so long since she'd let herself, she'd completely missed the signals.

It wasn't only that she found Liam attractive. She had a *crush* on him. The jiggly stomach, the lightheaded feeling she'd experienced as a sixteen-year-old girl. Not a thirty-three-year-old woman who had been around the block more times than the mailman.

This was not a problem, she told herself. She was not the irresponsible girl of her youth. She'd moved thousands of miles from home to lose her. To be free of the temptation. This was just a small setback.

And sitting in a dark auditorium ogling Liam for two hours was probably a really bad idea. At the same time, she wanted to be there for Papaw. He needed her support, her encouragement.

For the first time in a long time, she didn't know what to do. She hadn't anticipated this happening, so she didn't have a plan. A strategy. She felt out of control, and that scared the hell out of her because somewhere deep down, she liked it.

CLAIRE WAS ALREADY SITTING in the third row of the auditorium when Liam arrived at two for the second half of rehearsal. The cast was milling about on the stage. Frederick and Lily, he couldn't help noticing, stood on opposite sides.

"Liam!" Tracy called from the curtain. "Can you come here a minute?"

He hopped up on the stage and followed her to the left wing. She was holding one half of a broken compact disk. The rest of the disk and the plastic case lay shattered on the floor at her feet.

"It's the music for the show," she said.

"What happened?"

She shrugged. "I'm not sure. I just found it like this when I came back from lunch."

Last Liam had seen the CD, it had been lying on the prop table. How had it gotten all the way over here?

He knelt down to gather the pieces. Tracy may not have been the brightest crayon in the box, but she was a reliable assistant. She had no reason to move it, or lie if she had. And since CDs were not known to get up and walk around, or spontaneously shatter, he could only assume that it had been some sort of accident. Probably a few mischievous, unsupervised children playing where they shouldn't be.

"Did you see anyone back here?" he asked. "Before or after rehearsal this morning?"

"No one."

"Not to worry," he told her. "I have a copy in my cabin. It was probably just an accident."

She didn't look as though she believed him.

"To be safe, we'll keep a close eye on things," he said. "And Tracy, let's keep this to ourselves, okay?"

"Okay."

The last thing he needed was rumors that there were problems with the production. This was the first performance he had ever written, choreographed and produced entirely on his own. It had to be perfect.

"I heard that you volunteered to work with Frederick Miles," he said.

She shrugged. "He seemed to be having some trouble today at rehearsal. I thought he could use the extra practice."

Unfortunately, that was Liam's fault. It wasn't like him to stick his nose into other people's business, nor was he the type to play matchmaker, but for Frederick and Lily he was willing to make an exception.

They had both made a profound impact on his life. He wanted to return the gesture. With any luck they would settle their unfinished business.

"We're meeting an hour before rehearsal tomorrow," she said. "At his age, I don't want to overdo it."

And what better time to get those two together without the rest of the cast to distract them? "Have Lily join you."

"But she doesn't seem to be having a problem."

"Maybe not, but they're partners in several numbers. They need to learn the steps together." A very rational excuse.

"To be honest, Liam, I don't think they like each other much."

"Don't worry about that. Just teach them the steps."

She shrugged. "You're the boss."

It had taken a stroke of good luck, and a fair amount of arm-twisting, to get them both here together. This was a once in a lifetime opportunity and he wasn't going to let it pass them by.

CHAPTER FOUR

LILY WAS BEGINNING to believe that this trip had been a bad idea.

Despite Liam's assurances that it would be good for her, so far, nothing had been resolved. Skip had made his feelings regarding her presence very clear. After all these years she'd thought he might be ready to forgive her.

Maybe that was too much to hope for. As her father used to warn, maybe she should have let the sleeping dog lie.

From her table at the back of the dining room, and with a hollow heart, she watched the other actors all dining together. She might have joined them, but she was afraid of his reaction. She'd always hated being alone. Being isolated. Surely he remembered that. Maybe this was Skip's way of punishing her. And she was a fool for letting him. For caring what he thought.

Yet here she was, still sitting here, torturing herself. She would leave, eat dinner elsewhere, but she couldn't abide letting all of that food go to waste. Even though she hadn't done much more than push it around her plate.

They chattered and laughed, no doubt telling stories and anecdotes from the old days. Ones that most likely did not involve her. Her acting career had been short-lived and insignificant. A fluke, her first husband used to say. And wholly forgettable. Had she done things differently, chosen career over family, she wouldn't have gotten far, he had assured her. It had taken her years to realize he had been jealous of her success. But by then it had been too late. Her career had been too far gone to resurrect.

A warm hand curled over her shoulder and she jolted with surprise. She looked up to find Liam standing there, wearing his usual warm, sweet smile. And she needed a friendly face right now.

"Didn't mean to startle you." He leaned over and pressed a kiss to her cheek, then gestured to the empty seat beside her. "May I?"

She gave his hand a pat. "Of course, Liam, sit down."

He had grown to be such a handsome young man. Young to her anyway, though, goodness, he'd recently celebrated his thirty-fifth birthday, hadn't he? But he'd never lost that little-boy sweetness. Of all her great-nephews and -nieces on her second husband's side, Liam had always been her favorite.

They were very much alike, she and Liam. They understood each other. The fire that used to blaze inside of her, the one she'd doused to live up to her family's expectations, burned bright in Liam. She'd made it her mission in life to be an unconditional source of support and encouragement to him. She'd had no children of her own so he was something of a surrogate grandson to her.

Even more than that, he was her friend. She wouldn't let him make the same mistakes she had.

He stole a black olive from her plate and popped it in his mouth. "Rehearsal went well, I think."

Rehearsal itself. The before part couldn't have gone much worse.

And it was her own fault. The person she used to be, the gutsy girl from fifty years ago, would have marched right up to Skip and insisted he treat her with respect. But that girl was gone. She'd been exorcised from existence. By her parents and then a string of controlling husbands and failed marriages.

She missed that girl. Missed her very much.

Suppose she was still there somewhere? If Lily dug deep enough, would she find her buried beneath the burden of everyone else's expectations?

"I noticed the rest of the cast sitting across the room," Liam said, pilfering another olive. He might as well take the entire plate, she was no longer hungry.

There was a hollow loneliness taking up every bit of empty space inside of her. "I noticed them, too."

"Then why are you sitting here all by yourself?"

She wrung her napkin in her lap.

"Talk to me, Lily. Tell me what's wrong."

She looked up at him, recognized the sincerity in his eyes. He wanted so badly to help her. But she was afraid she might be beyond that now. "I think this was a bad idea, Liam. I feel as though I don't belong here."

"I must have heard you say a hundred times how you wished you could get the chance to see him again. To talk to him one more time. To finally make things right."

She may have said those things, but they had just been words. Wishful thinking. She'd never imagined Liam would take it to heart and go through all this trouble for her.

And now that he had, how could she tell him no? How could she admit her weakness without letting him down?

He wrapped her hands in his own, squeezing gently. He had to notice that they were shaking. "This is your chance, Lily."

"It's not the right time. I think they resent me being a part of the show."

"And I think you're imagining things." He was getting exasperated with her, she could hear it in his voice. And she didn't blame him one bit. She was acting like a coward.

"I'm a nobody has-been with two crummy pictures to my name. I'm out of my league."

"You're an *Academy Award–winning* actress with two *brilliant* films on your resume. You have just as much right to be here as they do. I know it's difficult, but you have to be brave."

She was tired of being brave. In fact, she didn't know if she had a scrap of courage left.

She glanced across the room to their table, relieved to see that people had already begun to leave. Dinner was over. She'd been spared.

She gestured toward the disbanding group. "I guess it will have to wait until tomorrow."

"Lily, I want you to promise me that tomorrow you'll sit with them."

"I will." But she wasn't sure that was a promise she was capable of keeping.

"I'm holding you to it," he warned, but the threat was uttered halfheartedly, because suddenly something else had caught his attention.

Skip's granddaughter, Claire.

She had risen from the table beside Skip and was leaving. And Liam watched, his look too intense to be casual curiosity. Not that Lily blamed him. She was a beautiful woman. The spitting image of her grandmother at that age.

Lily would never forget the day she'd opened the paper and read Skip and Marie's engagement announcement. Up until then, somewhere deep down, she'd held on to the hope that they would be reunited. She dreamed she would gather the courage to leave her husband for good. Her parents would see how much happier she was with Skip, and they would accept the marriage.

But Skip had fallen in love with someone else.

"She's very pretty," Lily said.

"She is," Liam agreed. He followed her with his eyes until she was through the door and out of sight.

Lily smiled. "I know that look, Liam. You like her."

He didn't confirm or deny her suspicions. He only smiled.

She wondered if Claire shared those feelings. Women found his boyish charm and sweet disposition irresistible—even though there hadn't been one yet who'd managed to tie him down. Liam wouldn't settle until he was good and ready.

Lily gave him a gentle nudge. "If you hurry, you could probably catch up with her."

"Are you trying to get rid of me?"

"Should I get up and shove?"

That one made him smile. "What if I said I would prefer to spend time with my favorite great-aunt-in-law instead?"

She smiled and patted his cheek. Such a sweet boy. "Then I would say that you're full of baloney. Besides, I'm going to turn in early. Rehearsal wore me out."

"That reminds me, we're starting an hour early tomorrow, so be at the auditorium by nine instead of ten."

"I can hardly wait."

He recognized the sarcasm, but let it slide. "Are you sure I can't interest you in a walk? A whirl on the dance floor? A game of Scrabble?"

"I'm sure. My old bones need rest. Claire on the other hand looks young and fit."

And if Claire was anything like her grandfather, she would be well worth the effort.

Which got Lily to thinking. If Skip was so worth the effort, what was she doing sitting here alone feeling sorry for herself? Why didn't she get off her duff and do something about it?

Huh, maybe there was a little of the old Lily left in there after all.

PAPAW WENT UP TO the room early, right after dinner, but Claire wasn't the least bit tired, and too restless to hang out in her room. She changed from her dinner dress into a soft linen pencil shirt and kimono sleeve blouse, then took a long walk on the deck.

Families played and couples walked hand in hand. Claire missed that sometimes. She missed feeling as though she was a part of something. Something other than work. But really, the nursery was her family now. Every summer when the college kids came looking for work, she became something of a surrogate older sister. When someone had a problem, personal or professional, she usually had advice to give. In her thirty-three years she had seen and done more than most people had in a lifetime.

Still, it wasn't the same as being close to someone. Really close. But letting down her guard, letting people in, came with dire consequences. If she didn't let people in, they couldn't hurt her.

How many times had she trusted Mira, only to be burned?

"I quit for good this time," Mira would tell her, and Claire would be sucked in by her mother's enthusiasm. By her own foolish hope. She would let herself believe that Mira had changed. Those brief periods of sobriety would last anywhere from a week to a month, then Claire would be back living in the spare bedroom of her grandparents' house because Mira couldn't "cope."

Eventually she'd learned to distance herself from Mira, to detach emotionally. Yet she always lived with the fear that she might be sucked back in, that one day she would let her guard down and Mira would weasel her way back into Claire's heart.

Avoiding Mira had become her only reliable defense. And when that failed to work, she'd tried rebellion instead.

Claire walked until the sun set and the air turned chilly, then she went back inside and browsed the boutiques and shops. She picked up a few souvenirs for her employees, and bought herself a pair of earrings to wear the night of the performance. One by one the shops closed, and all that was left open were the clubs.

There was one in particular, Vertigo, which was awfully reminiscent of the places she used to hang out in when she was younger. Younger and stupider. And she hadn't just hung out. She had lived in the bars and clubs, feasting on the atmosphere. Partying to her had been more than a lifestyle. It was an art form, and she was a master.

As she walked past the club doorway she stopped to peek inside. No fifties décor there. Colored lights flashed patterns on the ceiling and walls, and bodies in every shape and size bounced and gyrated on the dance floor. The heavy rhythm of music thumped through the floor under her feet, beckoning her, tempting her to wander inside.

How long had it been since she'd danced? Two years? Three? When was the last time she'd spent an evening out with people? And by people she didn't mean the theater board of directors or the garden club.

When was the last time she'd let loose and really had

fun? The temptation was almost irresistible, but she was stronger than that now. She continued on, returning instead to the coffee shop where she'd seen Liam that morning.

Not that she was looking for Liam. On a ship this big, what were the odds of them coincidentally bumping into each other twice in one day?

Nada.

Deliberately ignoring the seating section, she walked up to the counter and ordered herself a low-fat blueberry muffin and a decaf latte. She didn't usually eat sweets so close to bedtime, but what the heck, this was supposed to be a vacation. It was okay to break a *few* of the rules. The small, inconsequential ones.

She waited for her latte, itching to turn around. Just one quick, casual glance to find an empty table. And then she was struck with the undeniable sensation that someone was watching her.

You're being silly, she told herself. Even if he was there, and he happened to be looking at her, there was no way she could feel it. Despite living on an island that was known for its New Age mentality, she didn't believe in that kind of cosmic connection.

Then she heard a voice. *His* voice.

"Ms. Mackenzie, I could swear you're stalking me."

She refused to acknowledge the shiver of anticipation, the shudder of awareness that rattled through her like a four-point-five earthquake.

The clerk handed her the coffee, and with a ridiculously fluttering heart, she turned. Liam sat at a table in the corner, a paperback novel in one hand, a bottle of orange juice in front of him. An odd little jolt of surprise rocked through her when she realized he was dressed in jeans and a T-shirt. Out of costume he looked so normal. So casual and unthreatening.

So…*cute.*

Knowing she shouldn't, but wanting to anyway, she walked over to his table. If nothing else, this would give her a chance to ask him about Lily. And just like that she had the perfect excuse to justify spending more time with him. To not run shrieking in the opposite direction at the idea of spending time with a man she was undeniably attracted to.

He closed his book and grinned up at her—a genuine, happy-to-see-you smile—and gestured to the empty chair at his table. "You're on your own tonight?"

She slid onto the seat. "My grandfather turned in early. Rehearsal really wore him out."

"He did much better this afternoon, don't you think?"

Only when he wasn't around that Lily woman. Her presence was clearly upsetting him, and vice versa. Liam had to have noticed. But instead of separating them, he'd paired them up for three dance numbers.

She had tried to talk to Papaw about it again before dinner, but he'd remained tight-lipped. She wondered if Liam might know what was going on. "I think a lot of his trouble stems from that woman, Lily."

"What makes you think that?"

"You can't tell me you haven't noticed the tension between them."

He had this look, like he knew something he wasn't telling her. "I did notice. They have powerful chemistry."

"*Chemistry?*" Was he serious? "They act like they want to zap each other off the ship."

"I ran the risk of this happening when I invited them both here. But they need to do this. They both do."

All *that* told her was that he seemed to know what was going on, and she didn't.

"You look confused."

"That's because I am. Who is she? And how do they know each other?"

His brow tucked with concern. "Maybe you should ask him."

"I did. Several times. He refused to talk about it." And Liam's reaction was beginning to worry her.

"I'm not sure it's my place."

His *place?* A cold, sinking sensation filled her chest. How bad was it? "Please."

"Lily and Frederick were lovers."

Claire's heart bottomed out, sliding all the way to her stomach. *Lovers?* She had been guessing a past bad working relationship, or professional jealousy. Never had she dreamed he would accuse Papaw of infidelity.

She felt sick to her stomach. "That's not possible. He adored my grandmother. He would have never betrayed her." And if that wasn't true, she didn't want to know. In her entire life Papaw was the only man who hadn't lied to her or let her down.

She preferred to go back to being blissfully ignorant. "I don't believe it."

"I would never suggest such a thing. He was involved with Lily *before* he met your grandmother."

Her relief was overshadowed by shame. How jaded had she become that she could even think such a thing?

But if Papaw had had a relationship with this woman, why had she never heard about it? Why the big secret? As far as she knew, his life began with her grandmother. "They were serious?"

"They were engaged," Liam told her. "But she came from a strict Jewish family who refused to accept their relationship."

"Are you sure it's not just Hollywood legend? Rumors like this get spread all the time."

"I know it's true, because Lily is my great-aunt."

Knowing that Papaw had had a life before Grandma, that he had loved someone other than her, felt like a betrayal. Which deep down Claire knew was ridiculous, but she wasn't exactly thinking with her head right now. "They met on the set?"

He nodded. "They did two films together. They were small productions, but one earned her an Academy Award for supporting actress."

"Why only two movies?"

"You've heard of the McCarthy hearings?"

Anyone who lived in Hollywood knew of the hearings, the way Senator Joseph McCarthy used his influence to purge the industry of suspected communists. Anyone who refused to cooperate was blacklisted. "Of course. Papaw said it was an awful time, that so many good careers were ruined."

"Lily's was one of them."

"Was she a communist?"

"No, but she refused to testify. Back then, that was career suicide. Between that and the pressures from her family, she and your grandfather didn't stand a chance. And from what she's told me, they didn't part on good terms. I think they both have regrets."

"And you believe it's a good idea to dredge this up after all these years?"

"If they don't resolve this now, when will they?"

There had to be a catch. A reason this was so important to him. "What's in it for you?"

"Nothing but the peace of mind that I helped two people whom I greatly admire."

"I don't believe you." It was never that simple. *Everyone* had ulterior motives.

He shrugged. "I don't care what you believe."

His response stunned her for a second. Wasn't he going to try to convince her? Try to make her change her mind about him? Or was this some sort of twisted reverse psychology?

And what if he was right? What if Papaw and Lily really did need to resolve the past?

Liam gathered his things. "Well, I'd best be on my way."

She would have expected him to be angry with her, or at the very least, annoyed. Instead he spared her a polite smile, one that confirmed her opinion of him didn't mean squat, and rose from his seat. "Enjoy your evening, Claire."

She watched him walk away, feeling as though she had wronged him somehow. Which made no sense, seeing as how he didn't care what she believed. Not to mention the fact that she barely knew him, and had no intention of getting to know him any better.

Yet she couldn't help but recall something her grandfather had been telling her for years. Not everyone had ulterior motives. Sometimes what you see is what you get.

The problem was, she didn't trust her vision. It wouldn't be the first time her eyes had played tricks on her.

CHAPTER FIVE

AT NINE SHARP Frederick turned the corner by the auditorium door and nearly collided head-on with Lily.

"Watch where you're going!" he snapped.

She blinked with surprise and recoiled a step, as though she thought he might strike her.

What was wrong with him? What right did he have to treat her that way?

He already felt bad enough about dinner last night. She'd looked so lonely and small sitting all by herself. He should have invited her to join the rest of them. Instead he'd just sat there, waiting for...something. For her to make the first move, maybe.

Fifty years ago she would have walked up to the table, plopped herself down, and taken command of the conversation. The center of attention had always been her favorite place. She was young and bright and full of spirit. It could be exhausting at times, her endless energy and enthusiasm. She would act out a single scene fifty times without complaint if that's what it took to get it right.

He wondered what had happened to break her spirit.

Guilt had gnawed away at him all evening, robbing him of any enjoyment. It followed him back to his cabin and kept him tossing and turning most of the night.

Maybe she'd come by to give him a piece of her mind. The Lily he used to know wouldn't hesitate to put him in his place. The question was, how had she known he would be here early?

"What are you doing here?" he demanded.

His harsh tone made her wince. "I came for rehearsal."

"It doesn't start for another hour," he snapped.

Why was he being so rude? And why was she allowing it? Why wasn't she chewing his head off? Why didn't she tell him to go to hell?

He *wanted* her to fight him.

"I was told to be here at nine," she said.

"You must have heard wrong."

Finally something stirred beneath the humble facade. Something that resembled anger, or at the very least, a distant first cousin. "I hear just fine."

They reached for the door at the same time, bumping fingers. She yanked hers back, as though his touch repulsed her.

He pulled the door open and held it for her. "Go on, even though you'll just have to turn around and leave again."

Whatever bravery he saw in that instant, it was gone now. Her eyes lowered, she slipped past him. He followed her inside, up the center isle to the stage. Tracy was already there, warming up.

"Oh good, you're here!" she said when she saw them. "I'd like us to get started right away. We have a lot to learn and not a lot of time."

Why did she not look surprised to see Lily there?

"I think there's been a mistake," Frederick told her. "She's not supposed to be here."

"No mistake," Tracy said cheerfully. "Liam thought it best that you practice together, since you're going to be partners for several numbers."

Frederick looked at Lily and swore he could see the color drain from her face.

"*I'm* not having any trouble with the steps," she said.

Tracy shrugged. "Liam's the boss. I just do what he tells me to."

It wasn't in Frederick's nature to put up a fuss, so he held his tongue. He sort of hoped Lily would do it for him, but she just stood there, looking at her shoes.

"Let me go grab my script."

She disappeared backstage, and Frederick stood with Lily in awkward silence. Several minutes later when Tracy reappeared, she looked troubled.

Maybe she would cancel rehearsal, Frederick thought hopefully. "Is something wrong?"

"It's weird. I could swear I left my script back there, but it's gone." She shrugged. "Oh well. Liam probably grabbed it on his way out, thinking it was his."

"I guess we'll have to cancel," Lily said, confirming the fact that she was no happier to be here than he was.

"That's okay. We can just start with the second number. It's the one I'm most familiar with."

Damn, Frederick thought, and could see Lily was thinking the same thing.

They stood off to the side and watched as Tracy demonstrated the moves first, counting out the steps. A Fred and Ginger routine. Nothing he hadn't done before, albeit a long time ago.

So why did he feel so nervous?

So what if things hadn't worked out with him and Lily?

He'd had a good life. A happy marriage and a long and successful career. Given the chance to go back and change the past, he wouldn't do a single thing differently. So why was he having these feelings of regret?

It just wasn't meant to be. Isn't that what Lily had told him when she broke off the engagement? Hadn't it been *her* choice?

"Ready, Mr. Miles?"

At the sound of his name, Frederick blinked. Tracy was talking to him. "I'm sorry?"

"I said, are you ready?"

She'd been explaining the steps and he hadn't even been paying attention. He had no idea what he was supposed to do.

"Yes, of course I'm ready," he lied.

Lily stood there, waiting for him to get into position. With only a slight hesitation, he took her hand. It was cool and clammy and he could swear she was trembling. His other hand came to rest on her side. His heart rate increased tenfold and he felt beads of sweat break out across his forehead. He hadn't held Lily this way, hadn't touched her at all since the day she had told him goodbye.

"Okay!" Tracy called, clapping her hands. "Starting from the top. Five, six, seven, eight and step!"

He went right when he was supposed to go left and crashed into Lily, nearly knocking them both off balance.

She responded with an "Ooof!"

"Sorry," he mumbled. That was what he got for not paying attention.

"That's okay!" Tracy chirped. "Let's try it again! Just the way I showed you. Left foot first. Ready! Five, six, seven, eight and step!"

Left step, right step, left step. He was doing it. Left step, right…*on Lily's foot.*

She winced in pain and he mumbled another embarrassed apology.

"Good try!" Tracy called enthusiastically.

"Maybe you could show us again," Lily suggested, probably because she knew he would be too proud to ask.

"Of course!"

They stood to the side, and she went through the steps again, and this time he paid attention.

"Let's do that again," she said, "and be sure to watch your foot placement."

All right, old man, you can do this.

"Five, six, seven, eight and step!"

Step, step, swing. Step, step, spin. He had it this time. Step, step, swing.

Lily floated through the routine, her steps so light and airy she seemed to hover an inch above the floor.

"Good!" Tracy shouted. "Eyes forward, shoulders up!"

Step, step, spin—*crash.*

He knocked into her again.

"That's okay!" Tracey assured him. "That was *much* better."

"Getting a little rusty there, Skip," Lily said under her breath, and when he looked up at her, she had the shadow of a self-indulgent smile on her face. She was *enjoying* this.

Oddly enough, he would rather see her snap like an alligator than cower like a mouse.

Come on, old man, focus.

If she could do this, so could he.

He gripped her hand tighter, so hard he noticed her wince again. Fifty years ago, if he had pulled a stunt like that she would have driven the heel of her shoe into the top of his foot or kicked his shin.

"Again!" Tracy called. "And a five, six, seven, eight…"

He launched into the steps. Step, step, swing. Step, step, spin. He made it three-quarters of the way through before mis-stepping this time and tripping over her shoe.

Tracy clapped. "Awesome! It was much better this time! Let's try it again from the top!"

By the time the rest of the cast joined them at ten, he was doing much better. Not perfect, but he seemed to be adjusting to Lily's presence.

After rehearsal, Claire met him at the foot of the stage and gave him a warm hug.

"You were amazing!" she said, beaming with pride.

"I think *amazing* might be a bit of an exaggeration, but I am improving. What have we got scheduled for this afternoon?"

"The guest speaker luncheon starts in an hour, then there's an autograph signing afterward."

"I should probably get back to my room and shower."

"Do you have a minute to talk?"

"Of course, sweetheart. Is something wrong?"

"No. I just wanted to ask you about something."

The rest of the cast was already gone, so he gestured to a row of seats and they sat side by side.

"I want you to tell me about your relationship with Lily."

His denial was automatic. "What relationship?"

Claire wasn't buying it. "I know that you were engaged."

"Who told you that?"

"Do you deny it?"

He couldn't lie to her. "That was a long time ago. Before I met your grandma."

"I want to know why you've never told me about her."

She wouldn't understand. He was a different person back then. Times were different. "We were engaged, but it didn't work out. End of story."

"Why didn't it work out? What happened?"

He rose from his seat. "I have to go get ready."

He could feel Claire's eyes on him as he walked to the door. It hurt him to hide things from her, but if she knew the truth, what would she think of him?

Some things were better left in the past.

WHEN HER PHONE RANG, Tracy knew who it was. Salvatore was the only one who called her.

"Have you learned who has the pendant?" he demanded. He never even bothered to say hello. Never asked how she was. Because he didn't care.

He only cared about himself.

And he would be furious when he learned how little progress she'd made.

"It's only been two days," she said, sounding like a scared mouse. She hated that she couldn't stand up to him. That he made her feel so small and helpless.

"That's long enough," he growled. "What's taking so long?"

"I don't know who has the pendant. *No one* knows. Either it hasn't been found yet, or whoever did find it hasn't told anyone."

But of course that answer wasn't good enough for him. Nothing she ever did was good enough. "It never should have gone this far. You should have taken the pendant before that cruise director had a chance to hide it."

"It was in the safe. I couldn't get to it."

"I'm tired of your excuses!"

She opened her mouth to explain, but the words died in her throat. There was no point. It would only make him angrier.

"If you ever want to see your son again, you will find that pendant. You're running out of time."

At the mention of their boy, sick grief gripped her heart and squeezed, until it was difficult to breathe. She missed Franco so much that at times it was difficult to think straight, to be rational.

"How is he?"

"Like his mother. Always whining and complaining. He needs to learn to be a man."

Like you? she wanted to ask. You're not a man. You're just a bully. And she didn't want their son to be anything like him.

But she didn't dare say it.

"He's eating?"

"Of course he's eating! You think I would starve him?"

"No, I just…" Are you being good to him? she wanted to ask. Are you nice to him? But questions like that would make him angry. She could only hope the stern facade was to scare her, to motivate her to try harder. He wouldn't really hurt Franco. His own child. Would he?

Even Sal wasn't that cruel.

"Can I speak with him?" she asked.

"Why should I let you?"

"Please, Salvatore. I miss him so much."

He covered the phone and shouted to someone, probably one of his men, "Bring the boy to me."

Tracy waited, her heart in her throat, then she heard his sweet, angelic voice. "Hi, Mommy!"

"Hi, baby." She fought to keep her voice cheerful, so he wouldn't be afraid. "How is Mommy's precious boy?"

"I miss you, Mommy. When are you coming home?"

She could swear she felt her heart tear in half just then. "Soon, baby. I'll be home very soon. I promise. Mommy just has to work a little while longer."

On the outside she sounded calm, but on the inside she howled with despair and longing.

"Are you having fun with your father?" she forced herself to ask.

"I guess," he said but with little enthusiasm. She could picture him perfectly, standing with the phone pressed to his ear, his bangs in his eyes, his lip drawn into a pout. "I want to play outside, but Father says there are bad men."

Fear clutched her throat. Where were they? Had Salvatore taken him somewhere dangerous?

Even if he had, there was nothing Tracy could do about it. She had no idea where he was hiding Franco. A man like Salvatore had contacts all over the world. He could be anywhere.

"You listen to your father," she told him.

He sighed. "Okay."

He'd always been such a good boy. So obedient and sweet. He deserved so much better. Better than a father who was nothing more than a petty criminal in an expensive suit.

Sometimes she even wondered if Franco would be better off without her, too. Had she already failed him by getting involved with a man like Salvatore and his sleazy partner Kirk Rimstead?

"Tell your mother goodbye," she heard Salvatore order.

"Goodbye, Mommy," Franco dutifully supplied.

"Goodbye, baby. I love you!"

But Salvatore had already snatched the phone away. "Get the pendant," he threatened, "or that is the last time you'll speak to him. I'll tell him you died, then I'll take him to a place where you will never think to look."

Fear and grief threatened to swallow her up, but her voice sounded hollow and flat. "I will."

He disconnected and she set the phone down with shaky hands. In fact, she realized only now that she was trembling violently from head to toe.

Be strong, she told herself, brushing away the tears that escaped from her eyes. He needs you to hold it together.

Her parents had warned her that Sal was bad news, but he'd been charming to Tracy and made her feel beautiful. It didn't take long for her to realize that was all manipulation on his part, but by then it was too late. Sal and his partner Kirk Rimstead were experts at extortion. The pendant was supposed to be delivered to them by the former first officer Giorgio Tzekas for money he owed Sal—money he'd gambled away—but Giorgio had been arrested for dealing in stolen antiquities and the pendant left behind with its priceless diamond hidden inside. Somehow she always ended up in trouble, always tangled up with the wrong people.

This was the last time, she promised herself. She knew a man who could make documents. Passports, birth certificates. As soon as she got her son back, as soon as he was safe, they were going to disappear. They would get new names and go somewhere far away where Salvatore would never think to look.

And if she failed, if something happened to her baby, she would no longer have a reason to live.

CHAPTER SIX

CLAIRE HAD BEEN looking for a distraction. Something or someone to keep her mind off Liam. He introduced himself at dinner.

Ted from Seattle, on the cruise with his mother, Eleanor, one of the other guest actors from Papaw's era. He was a forty-one-year-old tax accountant, separated with two small kids. At a table of senior citizens it was nice to have someone closer to her own age to talk to, even if they had nothing in common but the burden of famous relatives.

Sure he was a little boring. All he talked about was his son and daughter, and unfortunately Claire had never been much of a kid person. He also had some major unresolved issues with his soon to be ex-wife. But he wasn't her type, and that made him safe.

After dinner Ted went back to his room to phone his kids and the seniors left to haunt a nightclub where they played big band tunes. Papaw invited Claire along.

"I'm exhausted," she lied, figuring the last thing he needed was a chaperone. And on the slim chance that Liam was right about Papaw and Lily needing closure—

not that she was ready to believe he was doing this out of the goodness of his heart—Claire didn't want to get in the way. "I'll probably turn in early. Don't forget we have that Panama tour tomorrow morning. The bus leaves at eight."

"Have fun tonight," he said, with a twinkle in his eye that had her wondering if he knew something she didn't. Maybe he thought she had a hot date. Or maybe he did. All that mattered was he seemed happy.

As she watched him walk away with his friends, she realized that for the second night in a row she was on her own.

Not that she wasn't used to being by herself. She might not have lived the most exciting life in the world, but on Saltspring Island she felt safe. Probably for the first time in her life. She showed people just enough of herself, as little or as much as she pleased, and no one pushed for more. Or even expected it. Everyone there seemed a bit on the eccentric side, slightly left of center. And because her life had never been what a person would call normal, that's probably why she fit in so well.

Since she had no intention of going back to her room this early, and going by the club was out of the question, she opted to explore instead. Unfortunately most of the shops had already closed for the night. Maybe it was inevitable, but eventually she found herself standing in front of the coffee shop.

She wasn't going to bother to pretend that she was having a coffee jones, or desperately needed a snack. Her mind had been telling her all day that she wanted to see Liam, and apparently her feet had been paying attention.

Not only was she craving his company, which in itself was strange enough, but she felt bad for the way she had acted the night before. Which was totally weird and unexpected considering she had trained herself not to care what other people thought.

What was happening to her? She knew the guy two days and all the defenses she'd worked so hard to build were coming crashing down around her. What made Liam any different than the other men in her life?

She stood outside the doorway wondering what she should do, but before she had the chance to make a definitive decision, she felt a funny little shiver of awareness. A second before he spoke, she knew Liam was standing behind her. The air felt charged with his presence.

"Why, Claire. Fancy meeting you here." Liam's voice, the lyrical patterns of his accent strummed across her skin like a caress.

"What are the odds?" She turned to him and the rhythm of her heart slammed into overdrive. He wore his retro uniform, and a charming, slightly arrogant grin. She knew that he knew this chance meeting was no accident.

"On your own again tonight?" he asked.

"My grandfather went dancing with his friends, but big band isn't really my thing."

He nodded toward the doorway. "Are you going in?"

"I was thinking about it. How about you?"

"Actually, I thought I might spend my break taking a walk on deck. Would you care to join me?"

Heck yes.

Come on, Claire, you could at least play a little hard to get. "Oh, I wouldn't want to disturb you while you take your break."

He folded his arms across his chest and gave her a slightly exasperated look and she knew exactly what he was thinking. If he didn't want her to, he wouldn't have asked.

She'd heard myths about men who actually said what they were feeling. She just didn't know they actually existed. But for some reason she had the feeling that, however rare a species he was, Liam was the real deal.

And for that, didn't she owe him an honest answer? She gathered her courage, inched her way a bit farther out onto the limb, and said, "I'd like that."

CLAIRE LEANED AGAINST THE railing and breathed in the warm, salt-scented air. It was dark and what had to be billions of stars lit the sky. A sound that she had yet to put a name to hummed in the air around her. So faint she wasn't sure if it was really there, but as fierce as a clap of thunder. She didn't know if it was natural or mechanical or a bit of both.

Liam stood beside her, his arms resting on the railing next to hers. They weren't touching, but she swore she could feel him. He could be ten feet away and probably still feel too close.

"I come out here quite often at night," he said, gazing out across the water. "It helps me clear my head."

She tried to imagine what it would be like, living on a ship. Being so cut off from the rest of the world. It was probably not unlike living on a small island.

"I owe you an apology, Liam."

He cast her a sideways glance. "For what?"

"Suggesting you had ulterior motives regarding Lily and my grandfather."

He shrugged. "You're certainly entitled to your opinion."

"Not if my opinion is based on assumptions. It's a lousy excuse, but where I grew up, people don't tend to do things out of the goodness of their hearts. Needless to say, I have some pretty major trust issues."

"Who doesn't have hang-ups and personality quirks? That's what makes us interesting."

He had a point. "Name one of yours."

Without hesitation he said, "I'm too honest."

"A man who's too honest?" She turned to look at him, to check for the hint of wry humor. But she could see that he was dead serious. "Wow. In my experience, most men wouldn't know the truth if it walked up and bit them in the butt. And you consider honesty a *bad* thing?"

"It can be."

She couldn't imagine how. "I'm going to need an example."

He thought about it for several seconds. "Suppose I told you that, since I met you, I haven't stopped fantasizing about kissing you."

Oh. My. God.

Her heart started pounding like crazy in her chest. She knew he was attracted to her, but to come right out and say it to her face? And would it be crazy to tell him she felt the same way? Unless he was only speaking hypothetically.

But it couldn't hurt to play along and see just where this might lead. "Suppose you did? What would be the consequences?"

He turned to face her, resting one arm on the railing, wearing a devilish grin. He knew exactly what she was doing, and he was having as much fun as she was. "You might be angry with me."

A day or two ago, maybe. But now? Not a chance.

She turned to him, mirroring his stance, aware that one step forward would bring them close enough to brush against one another. The idea sent a thrilling little shiver through her. "What if I only smiled?"

He leaned in, ever so slightly. She caught the scent of his aftershave, clean and masculine. "I would take that to mean that you want me to kiss you. In which case it would be rude of me not to."

This was no hypothetical scenario. She could see it in his eyes, the way he caught her gaze and held it, he was dead serious.

She'd forgotten how much fun this could be. The sexual innuendo and teasing. The anticipation of all the firsts. The first touch. The first kiss. Moments like these forced her to realize just how much she missed it. And she would give herself permission to indulge, if only for a little while.

"Still not seeing the problem," she said.

"The problem is…" he slid his hand along the rail until their fingertips touched "…one kiss would never be enough."

She couldn't argue with that. She felt herself leaning in, her body drawn to his like the pull of the tide to the shore. "So, you kiss me more than once. Big deal."

"Eventually, all that kissing is going to lead to other things."

She didn't have to ask what the *other things* would be. And she had never wanted a man to kiss her more than she did this very instant.

"And eventually," he continued, "someone will figure it out, at which point I will be looking for employment elsewhere."

"The no fraternization rule?"

"Exactly."

The idea of keeping their attraction a secret, of sneaking around, all the passionate stolen moments, made it that much more tempting. "Suppose we were careful? And we didn't get caught."

His fingers brushed over hers and every part of her hummed with anticipation. "That would be even worse."

"Why?"

"Because then we would fall in love with each other."

Fall in love? They barely knew one another.

She was beginning to see what he meant about total honesty not always being a good thing.

"That's quite an assumption," she told him. "Considering you barely know me."

"Maybe." He stroked the inside of her wrist with the pad of his thumb, and in spite of herself, a tiny gasp escaped her lips. "But you know it would be different with us."

He sounded so sure of himself. At the moment she didn't know who was nuttier. Him for suggesting it, or her for wanting to believe it.

His hand folded over hers, thumb teasing her palm. "I think we can agree that neither of us is looking for that."

Oh, man, he was good. He was seducing her with reverse psychology, tempting her with the forbidden fruit. All but daring her to prove him wrong.

"You're right, I'm not." She took a step back, pulling her hand from under his. "Although I still don't see why telling me the truth was a bad thing."

"Give it a day or two."

"For what?"

He only grinned. The radio on his belt squawked and a disembodied voice summoned Liam to the cruise director's office. "I guess that means my break is over."

"Well, it's been…interesting."

A wry grin tipped up the corners of his mouth. "That it has. Good night, Claire."

She watched him walk away, until he disappeared

inside, then she turned and leaned on the rail. As she bent forward the pendant slipped from inside her blouse and swung like a pendulum from her neck. She caught it in her fingers and rubbed the uneven surface. It was warm where it had been lying against her skin.

Was it a coincidence that for the first time in years she felt she had truly connected with a man? That while wearing the teardrop pendant, she'd begun to have *what might have been* thoughts? Or was it simply the power of suggestion?

She used to believe that some day she would meet the perfect man. They would get married and have kids—the normal stuff—and she would never take it for granted the way her own parents had. But as she got older and wiser, those dreams had grown more and more unrealistic, until they'd fizzled out altogether. Until she finally realized, there was no such thing as *normal*.

It was exhausting, always pushing people away. Sometimes she longed to give in. To connect. But at this point in her life, she was used to things the way they were. She didn't see a reason to change. She didn't have the energy.

Or maybe the truth was, she didn't have the courage.

WHEN HE SAW CLAIRE the next morning at the tour bus, Liam knew, without a doubt, she'd been thinking about him all night. He could see it in her eyes when she looked at him. At first, she wouldn't meet his gaze. Then, when she did, when their eyes locked and held, she looked torn between throwing herself into his arms and running back to *Alexandra's Dream* to hide.

She could deny it all she liked, try to convince herself he was mistaken, but deep down she knew he was right. It would be different for them, if their timing hadn't been so lousy.

"Sleep well?" he asked, not doubting for an instant that the dark circles under her eyes were largely due to their conversation last night.

She sucked in a chest full of hot, dusty air and shot him a wry, *What do you think?* look. "And you?"

She already knew the answer. "Did you find what you were looking for?"

She looked confused. "Huh?"

"Your grandfather said you ran back to the cabin to grab something that you forgot."

"Oh, yeah." She touched the front of her T-shirt, as though the item he referred to was hidden beneath it. "I did, yes."

"Let's get a move on, then. We're already a few minutes behind schedule." He gestured to the bus and waited for her to climb on.

She took a seat beside her grandfather and Liam settled in near the front. The bus pulled away from the dock, bumping along to the main road.

As they began the short drive to the Panama Canal, Liam was amazed by the acute level of tension between Frederick and Lily. Claire's grandfather had been doing a stellar job of ignoring Lily, who sat with Eleanor and was doing an equally impressive job of pretending Frederick didn't exist.

The *Minaflores* visitor's center sat high on an embankment overlooking the canal. As they climbed a massive set of steep, concrete steps, Lily attached herself to Liam.

"You two aren't fooling anyone," Liam whispered. "You're the two most stubborn people I've ever known."

Lily looked up at him, one brow arched. "Look who's talking, Mr. I-can't keep-my-eyes-off-Claire."

He shrugged. "I don't deny it."

She huffed and rolled her eyes, but he knew that she knew he was right.

A guide met them in the lobby and launched into a tour of the Canal operations. Four exhibition halls, organized by themes, elaborated the history of the Canal, the importance of water as a source of life, the Canal's operation, and its crucial role in world trade.

They spent the next hour browsing displays of Canal operations, interactive modules, video presentations and models. But Liam found his attention wandering to Claire instead. In an army-green T-shirt and khaki shorts, her hair pulled back in a ponytail and her face free of makeup, she had something of a tomboyish look about her.

Though he had nothing against the vintage fashions he'd seen her wearing until now, he couldn't help thinking she looked more natural this way.

They filed out onto a large balcony overlooking the Canal's three sets of locks to watch the opening and closing of the miter gates as ships passed through. Claire stood off to herself, leaning on the railing. Then she cast a backward glance at him over her shoulder, as though beckoning him.

"I think I'll take a run to the ladies' room," Lily said, giving him a nudge. "Go talk to her."

Lily disappeared through the crowd of tourists and Liam joined Claire at the rail.

"Enjoying the tour?" he asked.

"Okay, you were right." She glanced over at him. "Happy?"

"That depends on what it is I was right about."

"The whole honesty thing." She dropped her voice to a whisper. "I can come up with a dozen reasons why getting involved would be a total disaster."

"Only a dozen?"

She glanced around to be sure that no one from their group was nearby. "So why is your kissing me all I can think about? Why is it that when you're around, I can feel you there even before I see you?"

At least he wasn't the only one.

"You know we can't do this," she said.

Yes, he knew that. That knowledge however made it no less tempting. But Liam had no interest in being tied down. Not yet. Life was a series of adventures, and he had barely scratched the surface. There was still too much to do and see, too many experiences he might miss out on. "You're absolutely right," he agreed.

His answer seemed to surprise her. "I am?"

"Sadly, yes." But they would have been good. And not finding out how good would be one regret he would have to learn to live with.

"That's it? You're not going to try to change my mind?"

"I'm not."

She studied him for a minute, then smiled. "Okay. I get it. I see what you're doing."

"What am I doing?"

"You think that telling me it can't happen will make me want it even more."

He wished that had been his intention. "You're forgetting one thing. I never say anything I don't mean." Liam checked his watch and saw that it was getting late. They had more places to see and the senior citizens were bound to get tired soon. "Could you help me gather the group, so we can be on our way?"

Was that disappointment he saw as she headed off to locate the members of the tour? Did she want him to pursue her?

Or perhaps she wasn't sure what she wanted.

After a tour of the art museum in *Las Bovedas,* a walk through the famed Santo Domingo Church, and finally a bus ride through the banking district, the elderly members of the group dragged themselves back onto the ship, looking in desperate need of a nap. Liam overheard Frederick telling Claire that he was going up to his room.

"I'll be down for dinner," he told her. "And don't forget about the movie screening this evening. You promised to be my date."

"I'll walk you up," she said. No doubt to run interference. Liam had seen the way the passengers flocked around him and Frederick looked to be in no shape to sign autographs and chat with adoring fans. And sure enough, as they headed to the elevator, people began to whisper amongst themselves and gravitate in their direction.

Claire took her grandfather's arm, as if to rush him along, but there was no way they would be able to outrun the fans. And as assistant cruise director it was Liam's duty to see that the special guests were gently steered from harm's way.

Liam took off after them and caught up just as they were stepping onto the elevator. He entered behind them, effectively blocking the way, and was met with a dozen disappointed faces. "Mr. Miles will be signing autographs in the lounge after the screening this evening," he said, then tapped the button to close the doors. When they were moving he turned to Claire and her grandfather.

They both looked a bit surprised by his arrival.

"I have business on the Artemis deck," he explained, but he could see Claire wasn't buying it. She didn't look any less grateful though. And her poor grandfather appeared ready to collapse.

The doors opened to the Artemis deck and Liam escorted them down the blessedly deserted hall to Frederick's room.

"I'll see you both this evening," the older man said, kissing Claire's cheek.

"Have a good nap, Papaw." After her grandfather stepped inside and shut the door, she turned to Liam, sporting a wry grin. "You didn't really have business on this deck, did you?"

"Seeing that your grandfather made it safely to his room *was* my business."

"Well, thank you. He's always had a tough time saying no to his fans. Who knows how long we might have been stuck there."

"The tour took a lot out of him."

"He'll feel much batter after a nap."

They turned and walked toward the elevator together. "I'm curious, where does the term 'Papaw' come from?"

"According to my grandmother, when I first started talking, I couldn't say grandpa. I said Papaw and it just sort of stuck, I guess."

A lock of hair had slipped from her ponytail and lay against her cheek, and Liam had the almost irresistible urge to reach up and smooth it back behind her ear. He wouldn't of course, but that knowledge didn't make him want to do it any less.

They reached the elevator and she pushed the button. "As a thank-you for watching out for us, could I buy you a cup of coffee?"

Liam, old chap, that would be a very bad idea. "No thanks necessary."

"Can I buy you one anyway?" She gazed up at him through a curtain of thick dark lashes and he could feel his resolve melting away.

But really, what was the harm in *one* cup of coffee?

The elevator doors opened and he gestured inside. "After you."

CHAPTER SEVEN

"I FEEL STRANGE being out of costume," Claire said as they got in line at the coffee shop behind a greaser and a girl in vintage cheerleading getup. "Maybe I should have changed back into my fifties clothes."

"Not to worry, you won't be expelled from the cruise," Liam teased. "Dress code participation is mandatory only for the staff." And even then they were given some leeway.

The fraternization regulation on the other hand was carved in stone. But he never had been the type to play by the rules.

Claire reached up to touch whatever it was she had hidden beneath her shirt.

"Can I ask you a question?" Liam said. "Something that's been nagging me all afternoon."

She nodded, moving forward with the line.

"What was it that you went back for this morning?" She looked confused, so he added, "Before you got on the bus. You said you found what you were looking for, then touched something underneath your shirt. All morning I noticed you fiddling with it. Just the way you are now."

"I didn't realize I was doing that." She reached underneath the collar of her shirt, producing a familiar silver pendant.

"Ah, so you're the lucky guest. Everyone was wondering where it had disappeared to. Tracy must have asked me a dozen times if I knew who found it." He held out his hand. "May I?"

She slipped it over her head and handed it to him. Up until now, he'd only seen it in the brochure. It felt heavy in his hand and warm from her body heat. "So this is what all the fuss is about. Not much to it, is there?"

"Personally, I think it's kind of clunky. But I promised Papaw I would keep it with me. He seems to have the idea that it's lucky."

"So they say. Everyone who has worn it so far claims to have benefited from its so-called magical powers. The wearer is supposed to get special treatment from the staff, too."

Liam heard a gasp, and they both turned to see Tracy standing in line behind them. "Speak of the devil. I was just telling Ms. Mackenzie how interested you are in the pendant hunt."

Tracy had the oddest look on her face just then. A combination of surprise and uneasiness. But she quickly hid it behind a smile. "Congratulations," she told Claire.

Claire backed up a step. "You're not going to break into song or something, are you?"

Tracy looked confused. "Break into song?"

"The special treatment I'm supposed to get for having found the necklace."

Tracy giggled, but it came out forced and awkward. "No, of course not. But if you show it at the counter you might score a free coffee." She turned to Liam. "I need to talk to you. *Now.*"

Looked like the coffee would have to wait. He handed the pendant back to Claire and she slipped it into her purse. "I'm afraid you'll have to excuse me, Claire. Can I get a rain check on that coffee?"

She actually looked disappointed. "Of course."

"By the way," Tracy said, "I wanted to tell you how nice it's been working with your grandfather. He's really sweet."

Claire beamed. "Thank you. He's had very nice things to say about you, too. I appreciate the time you're taking to help him."

Tracy flashed her plastic smile. "We should sit and chat sometime. Get to know each other."

Here we go again, Liam thought. She seemed to do this every cruise. Attach herself to one of the guests and as a result begin neglecting her duties.

"Sure," Claire said, a bit unenthusiastically. He gave Tracy's sleeve a subtle tug and she followed him out the door.

"Messing around with a guest?" she asked when they were out of earshot.

"Not anymore," he joked.

"You'll get fired." He could swear she almost sounded worried about him.

"We were having coffee. Nothing more. I do appreciate the concern though."

"Patti can be a real tyrant. She acts like a human being when you're around. If you get fired, where does that leave me?"

So she wasn't worried about his career per se, just the quality of her own working environment. He couldn't really say he was surprised. "So, why the urgency?"

"Have you been backstage today?"

"I had a tour this morning. I haven't been in the auditorium since yesterday after practice. Why?"

"Come on. You have to see this to believe it."

LIAM WAS UPSET ABOUT something.

Claire watched from her seat in the third row, wondering what could be wrong. She'd thought it was a little strange that he'd been MIA at the screening and the after party in the lounge. And yes, she'd felt disappointed.

He hadn't smiled a single time since rehearsal started an hour ago, and he seemed to lack his characteristic enthusiasm. It felt almost as though he was going through the motions, biding his time until he could escape.

Partway through practice, Patti, the cruise director, showed up. She and Liam stood off to the side talking for several minutes. It was no friendly, lighthearted conversation, either. Something was going on.

Claire wondered if it had anything to do with what Tracy had come to tell Liam in the coffee shop.

Liam asked Tracy to take over and disappeared with Patti backstage. Several minutes later she emerged without Liam. She spoke to Tracy for a second, then hopped down from the stage and headed in Claire's direction.

Had Claire done something wrong?

"Ms. Mackenzie, how are you enjoying your cruise?"

"It's been great. I was a little apprehensive about the costumes, but it's turned out to be a lot of fun."

"I understand that you've been sitting in on rehearsals."

Maybe Patti had figured out that she was mostly there to see Liam, and he had gotten in trouble. "Is that a problem?"

Patti blinked with surprise. "Why, no, of course not. I just wanted to be sure you understand that you don't *need* to be here. Your grandfather is in good hands."

The same hands she wished *she* was in. Liam's. "My grandfather and I don't get to spend much time together these days. It's nice to just be close to him."

Patti smiled, a very warm, genuine smile. "He's very lucky to have you here with him."

"I'm the lucky one, Ms. Kennedy. My grandfather is very special."

"I can see that. We appreciate him taking the time to attend the cruise. If there's anything you or Mr. Miles need, anything at all, ask Liam and he'll see that it's taken care of."

Anything? Claire wondered.

"*Ms. Kennedy,*" a deep, male voice purred from the auditorium door. "I need to speak with you."

Claire turned in the direction of the voice, found that its owner was the absolute epitome of tall, dark and handsome. He seemed wrapped in sizzling sex appeal.

Patti didn't even look. She just closed her eyes and took a deep breath, as though summoning her patience. "Thanasi Kaldis," she told Claire. "The hotel manager. Will you excuse me?"

"Of course."

Patti walked to the door, her spine so rigid, her body so tense, Claire thought for a second that she might haul off and deck him. She wondered what was going on between those two.

Rehearsal ended several minutes later, but Liam hadn't returned, and frankly the curiosity was killing Claire. She was also just the tiniest bit worried. She waited around until the entire cast had left, including Tracy, but still no Liam. She was about to give up when she heard banging from backstage.

Someone was there.

She walked down the aisle and boosted herself up on the stage. It had been a long time since she'd been on a stage for any reason. It used to be a typical part of life—theaters, studio back lots, television production sets. She'd been to them all. There were times when she sort of missed that part of her life, but mostly she was glad it was over.

She followed the sound of pounding behind the curtain. There she found Liam, tossing tools into a toolbox, each landing with a loud clang.

"What did those tools ever do to you?" she asked.

He spun around, hammer raised in mid-toss. She

took a step back for fear that he might lose his grip and clobber her.

"Sorry," he said, dropping the hammer with a loud thud. "You startled me."

"I didn't mean to."

He looked around uneasily. "What are you doing back here?"

"I heard all the banging and thought I better check it out."

"Well, it's nothing."

She had the distinct impression he was trying to hide something. She folded her arms across her chest. "Are you trying to get rid of me?"

She expected a smile, but he remained solemn. "In fact, I am."

Now she was getting worried. "Liam, what's wrong? Did you get fired or something?"

He dragged his hands down his face. "It's better that you don't get involved."

Involved? What the hell was that supposed to mean? "Too late. I'm already involved. And I'm not going anywhere until you tell me the truth."

"You can't tell anyone," he warned her. "You have to swear to it."

"I swear."

"I mean it, Claire. Not a soul. If what I'm about to show you gets out, it could put an end to the production."

This was serious. "I won't tell anyone. I swear."

Liam walked to the side of the stage and lowered the backdrop.

When she saw the front, she gasped. On the surface was a beautifully painted representation, a colorful collage of all the notorious Hollywood hot spots, the way they would have looked in the 1950's.

The bottom eight feet or so had been slashed and hung in ruins. "Who would do this?"

He shrugged, looking hopelessly baffled. "Patti has security looking into it."

She could see then, in the despair on his face, how much this show meant to him, and it touched her somewhere deep inside. And since she didn't know what else to do, she stepped up beside him, and for a minute they stood there together in total silence staring at what was left of the backdrop.

"What now?" she asked.

"There's no time to have it repainted, and I can't imagine how we would fix it." He shook his head in disgust. "So we have the show with no backdrop. The cast is going to be so disappointed. I wanted to create a show they could take pride in."

"Liam, I'm sure they'll understand that this isn't your fault."

"Patti is going to try to find a replacement, but it might be too late." He tugged the backdrop up and out of sight. "There have been other things," he admitted. "But on a much smaller scale."

Her heart sank. "Describe smaller."

"A broken CD. A missing script. Petty inconveniences."

"Until now."

He nodded. "If all the incidents *are* linked, whoever is doing this is getting more destructive. Which is why it's imperative that this is kept quiet until we figure out what's happening. Patti is afraid that if word of this gets out, it might frighten people away."

"And what's going to stop this person from making more trouble?"

"All the doors leading in or out of the auditorium will remained locked at all times except rehearsal." He looked up to where the remains of the backdrop hung. "So much for jump-starting my career as a director and choreographer."

She didn't know why that should surprise her, since it was exactly what he was doing here. "You want to choreograph and direct?"

"And teach. At least, that was the plan. It was an amazing stroke of luck that I landed this position."

"What about performing? Dancing and singing? You're so talented."

He cracked a smile. "Thank you. But I'm thirty-five years old. There comes a point when you have to step aside for the younger generation."

"If choreographing and directing is what you really want, you won't let a small setback get in your way."

His smile widened. "Claire, I do believe you like me."

Well, duh. He was only now figuring that out? Instead of answering, she looked at her watch. "Wow, I didn't realize how late it is. I don't want to miss lunch, or the beach party out by the pool this afternoon. Will you be attending?"

He let her obvious diversion slide. "I'm afraid I can't."

That's too bad. She would have given anything to see him in a Speedo.

"Maybe later we can get that cup of coffee," he suggested instead.

"Maybe we can." As she walked to the auditorium door, she could feel his eyes following her. Deep down in her bones, she knew this flirting thing they were doing was a mistake. Despite agreeing that they couldn't have any sort of relationship, they'd already set the gears in motion. But for the first time in a long time, she was having too much fun to care.

FREDERICK WAS BEGINNING TO worry about Claire, then just as lunch began she appeared at their table.

"Sorry I'm late," she told everyone, sliding into the empty chair beside him, her cheeks rosy, eyes bright. She was cheerier than usual. Almost giddy, and he couldn't help but wonder what she'd been up to.

He'd waited for her outside the auditorium earlier. When several minutes passed and she hadn't come out, he went back in to look for her but she was already gone. He wasn't sure where she could have disappeared to, but it was obvious she was up to something. And he was pretty sure that something was named Liam.

Liam was a fine fellow. Responsible and polite. And he had feelings for Claire—Frederick could see that. Even if it was only for a week, he was just the sort of man Claire needed. Someone to coax her back into the land of the living, to teach her that it was all right to have fun. Someone to trust, so she might just begin to trust herself.

And for that Frederick forgave Liam's meddling in his personal life.

Eleanor had let it slip that Lily was Liam's great-aunt by marriage. Lily had no doubt disclosed that fact in confidence, but Eleanor had never been much good at keeping a secret.

Frederick was positive this wasn't an innocent case of nepotism. Liam had asked them both on the cruise for a precise reason.

Unfortunately he'd wasted everyone's time. Frederick wanted no part of this reconciliation. The past was the past as far as he was concerned. Anything between them that needed resolving had been settled in his mind a long time ago.

Frederick had moved on, and it was time Lily did the same.

"I KNOW WHO HAS IT," Tracy told Salvatore excitedly.

"Who?"

"Her name is Claire Mackenzie."

"I won't be satisfied until it's in my hands," he said, not impressed with her good news.

"But I'm friends with her grandfather." She knew that calling Frederick Miles a friend was a bit of a stretch, but she would say anything to assure him. "I'll get it this time. I promise I will."

"Your promises mean nothing to me."

She felt her high spirits begin to sink, but she refused to let him get the best of her. "Can I talk to Franco?"

"When I have the pendant, you may talk with your son. Not a moment before."

Her heart twisted in her chest. She couldn't help but notice that he called Franco *her* son. Didn't he have any feelings for his own child? Was he nothing more than a bargaining chip?

"I'll get it this time, I swear I will."

"You've failed me twice already. If there is a third time, you *will* be sorry."

The line went dead. She set the phone down, her hands trembling. She could not mess this up. Whatever it took, she would do it.

She experienced a strange feeling of lightness in her chest and realized that it was hope. Despite Sal's doubt in her, she knew she would do it this time. She would get the pendant and get her son back.

Now all she needed was a plan.

CHAPTER EIGHT

GOD, SHE WAS PATHETIC.

Claire sat near the rear of the coffee shop, sipping the cold dregs of her mocha latte, stealing glances at her watch and feeling like the world's biggest moron.

Forty minutes she'd waited, and finally concluded that Liam wasn't coming. The only thing worse than her shame was the sharp sting of disappointment.

She had been looking forward to this all day. Every time she turned a corner she had hoped to see him standing there. All afternoon she had deliberately haunted areas of the ship where she thought he might be.

Totally pathetic.

Well, she wouldn't make the same mistake twice. She rose from her chair, tossed her empty cup into the trash receptacle and headed up to her room. She was both surprised and relieved to see a dim glow from the bottom of her grandfather's door. He was supposed to be out dancing with his friends.

She knocked lightly and called, "It's me, Papaw."

"Come in," he called, so she used the spare card key he'd given her.

He was sitting in bed wearing his cotton pajamas, a paperback book in his lap. "Hello, sweetheart."

She tossed her purse on the love seat and kicked her sandals off, then sat at the foot of his bed and curled her feet underneath her. "No dancing tonight?"

"I'm exhausted. The beach party took a lot out of me. I must have signed a hundred autographs." He folded the corner of the page he'd been reading and set the book on the bedside table. "What about you? I thought you had plans tonight. It's barely ten o'clock. Why aren't you out having fun?"

There was no one to have fun with. Of course, that never would have stopped her before. She hadn't been shy about introducing herself to people, making new friends.

And she had been just as accomplished at losing them.

She shrugged, too embarrassed to tell him the truth. That she'd been stood up. "You up for a game of rummy?"

"Maybe tomorrow, sweetheart."

"Why don't we just talk, instead?"

"What did you want to talk about?"

"Tell me about Lily."

Up went the hackles and down came the shield. "What about her?"

She rose up on her elbows. "Don't even try to pull that with me."

He wouldn't look her in the eye. "Surely someone has told you by now."

"I want to hear it from you."

He stared at her, lips sealed in defiance. If that was the way he wanted to play this, fine.

"If you won't tell me, I'll just have to ask Lily."

His eyes narrowed. "Stay away from her."

"What choice do I have when you refuse to talk to me? I want to know about your life, Papaw. You're not going to be around forever. Would you just let your past die with you?"

That seemed to snag a nerve. "I don't like to talk about it. It was a long time ago."

"You loved her," Claire said. Not a question, but a fact. All he had to do was confirm or deny.

After several seconds he nodded.

"But it didn't work out," she coaxed. "She chose her family over you. Right?"

"Something like that."

"And you never spoke to her again?"

"Never."

He looked so sad, it broke her heart. "Why not?"

"I met Grandma not long after and knew immediately we were meant to be together. She was my soul mate."

"But you never forgot Lily, did you?"

"It all worked out for the best. What difference does it make now?"

"It makes a huge difference." She knew this was going to be a tough sell, but she could at least try. "If you and Lily had stayed together, if she had chosen you, what do you think would have happened?"

He shrugged. "How should I know?"

"Hypothetically speaking. Would it have worked out?"

He was quiet for a full minute and she thought for sure he was going to shut her out again. Finally he said, "Things were different back then. Jews didn't marry Catholics."

She wasn't buying it. "If they loved each other they did."

"We had too many differences of opinion."

"Differences of opinion?" She'd been hoping for answers, but she was more confused now than when she'd walked in the door. And angry. "Why can't you just level with me? Tell me the *truth*."

"The truth is…" He lowered his eyes to his lap. "We were both at fault. I let her down and she never found it in her heart to forgive me."

Finally. A straight, honest answer. "And all these years later you still regret it."

He looked so sad. Sad and weary. "I have many regrets, sweetheart."

"But this is one you could resolve. And you could start by admitting you still have feelings for her."

"And how do you know that?"

"Because you spend so much time pretending that you don't. Why don't you just talk to her? You could at least be friends."

"I have plenty of friends. I don't need any more."

She'd always considered Papaw easygoing and down-to-earth. Who knew he could be so pigheaded.

"You must have told me a million times that I inherited my stubborn streak from Grandma, but I think it came right from you."

With an exaggerated yawn he stretched. "Boy, I'm exhausted. Time for some shut-eye."

"Papaw—"

"I'll see you in the morning." He reached over and switched off the lamp beside the bed, plunging them into total darkness.

At least she'd made a little headway.

She sat there listening in the darkness, and when his breathing became slow and deep—he was either sleeping or pretending to be—she slipped out of his room and into her own.

She hoped he would have the good sense to take this opportunity to settle things with Lily. It probably should have been Papaw who'd found the pendant, she thought wryly. Not that it had done her much good today.

She reached up to feel it resting under her shirt, and realized it wasn't there.

Had she lost it?

In a brief moment of panic, her eyes swept the room. Then she remembered taking it off to show Liam, and dropping it into her purse afterward. She checked and sure enough, that was where she found it, coiled in the bottom beneath her hairbrush. She'd gone a day and a half not wearing it.

Could that be the reason for her crummy afternoon?

Oh, my God.

She rolled her eyes at the sheer ridiculousness of her thoughts. It was a necklace, for heaven's sake.

But she had promised Papaw she would wear it, so she slipped it over her head. The instant the weight of the pendant hit her chest, someone knocked at her door.

Who could it be at this hour?

Wouldn't it just be the weirdest thing ever if it was Liam, there to apologize and explain why he stood her up?

Now she was being ridiculous.

The odds of it being Liam on the other side of the door were about one in a thousand. And besides, he didn't owe her an explanation. It was never even a set date. Just something mentioned in passing.

Grow up, Claire.

She tugged the door open, her jaw dropping when she saw who stood on the other side.

Liam smiled back at her. "Surprise."

If that wasn't the understatement of the century. She managed to choke out a weak, "Hey."

He was dressed like a greaser, complete with the ducktail do and leather jacket. "I know it's late. I hope I'm not disturbing you."

"Of course not."

"I just wanted to apologize."

Play it cool, she warned herself, when on the inside she was doing cartwheels. "For what?"

"For standing you up. I got roped into covering for one of the dancers. I didn't even have time to call and leave you a message."

She put on her confused face. "Did we have plans?"

He leaned against the doorjamb, arms folded across his chest. "Coffee."

"Oh, right," she said, so smooth. "Was that *tonight?*"

A grin tipped up the corner of his mouth. "Funny you don't remember. The girl behind the counter said that you spent almost an hour waiting for me."

Oh, busted.

She shrugged. "Maybe I was waiting for someone else."

"There's another assistant cruise director on this ship named Liam? Because that's who you told her you were waiting for."

Damn, she'd forgotten about that.

"I am sorry," he said, and she got that warm, fuzzy feeling all over. "I'd like to make it up to you."

Oh, man, could she think of several ways he could make it up to her. *Invite him in,* her subconscious chanted. *Give him a chance to let him show you how sorry he is.*

Claire, get your mind out of the gutter.

She was not that girl any longer. The one who slept with men she hardly knew just to feel special. To feel loved. But it was never about love.

"Coffee, tomorrow morning?" he asked.

Even better. No one got their heart broken drinking coffee. "Sounds good."

"Seven-thirty?"

"I'll be there."

For a moment he just stood there looking at her, wearing that quirky smile.

For an instant she wondered if he was going to kiss her. The idea thrilled her and scared her half to death.

He reached up with his right hand, paused for a split second, then brushed the top of one finger across her cheek. Light as a feather on a resting bird's wing. Her knees went weak and nearly bucked out from under her, and her head started to swim in a sudden estrogen flood.

He held it there for several long seconds, then dropped his hand and smiled. "See you in the morning."

She uttered a reply that to her sounded like nonsensical babble, then shut the door. She leaned against it, feeling weak and shaky all over.

That brief, simple touch had been more tantalizing, more passionate than any kiss she remembered.

She wanted Liam. *Really* wanted him.

Oh, man, was she in trouble.

THIS COULD NOT HAPPEN to her twice.

Claire sat in the coffee shop waiting. *Again.* It was seven-fifty and no sign of Liam. Why did she do this? Why torture herself this way?

And so much for the pendant being lucky.

In a huff, she snagged it from around her neck and dropped it on the table beside her cooling coffee, mumbling, "Stupid piece of junk."

"Everything okay?"

Claire looked up to see Tracy standing beside the table. She forced a smile. "Fine. Thanks."

Uninvited, the dancer slid into the empty seat across from Claire. "I do that, too, sometimes."

Claire wasn't exactly in the mood for company, but she had to ask. "Do what?"

"Talk to myself when I'm mad about something. Or someone." She nodded to the pendant. "I thought that was supposed to be good luck."

"Me, too."

"Maybe it's ready to…I don't know, *move on*. Maybe if one person keeps it too long, it becomes bad luck."

That was even more ridiculous than the idea of it being good luck. Still she shrugged and said, "Maybe."

"I can take it for you. Give it back to Patti."

Claire was tempted, since it didn't seem to be doing her much good. But then Papaw would eventually notice it was gone, and despite his recent stubbornness, she didn't want to disappoint him.

"Thanks." She scooped the necklace up and dropped it back in her purse. "But I think I'll hang on to it."

Tracy's cheeks flushed, two bright red spots, and she lowered her eyes to her lap. Claire could swear she was about to burst into tears. Why had she even sat down?

"Did you need something?" she asked.

Tracy frowned. "Need something?"

"I was just wondering why you sat down at my table."

"Oh, right!" She shook her head and giggled nervously. "I almost forgot."

"Forgot what?"

"Liam asked me to find you."

"Oh." Her heart did a quick back and forth shimmy. "What did he want?"

"He said to tell you that he's not going to be able to make it for coffee. One of the dancers fell during routine rehearsal this morning and hurt her back. She was pretty freaked out, so Liam is staying with her in the infirmary."

That had to be one of the sweetest things Claire had ever heard. And she felt like a slime for being angry with him. She should have known he would have a logical excuse for not being here. Because Liam never said anything he didn't mean.

She truly believed that.

"Will she be okay?" she asked Tracy.

"They're doing X-rays right now."

"It's nice of Liam to stay with her."

She shrugged. "You like him, don't you?"

"Like him?" She was treading on dangerous ground. She didn't know the level of Liam and Tracy's friendship. Or if they even were friends. She didn't want to inadvertently get him fired.

Tracy grinned. "I won't tell anyone. I just want you to know, he's okay. I've worked with some major sleazebags over the years. Liam is one of the good guys."

"I can see that."

"You know that if he gets caught messing around with you, he'll lose his job."

"Tracy—"

"I know, it's none of my business. I should butt out." She rose to her feet. "I almost forgot. Liam wanted to know if you would be at rehearsal this afternoon."

She wouldn't miss it. "Tell him I'll definitely be there."

AFTER TWO DAYS AT SEA, Claire's legs felt squishy and unsteady as she walked the ramp into the Costa Rican Port of Limon. A wave of brutally hot and humid air nearly stole the breath from her lungs. She gave herself a minute to adjust, then breathed in the scents of the tropical terrain. Towering palm trees swayed over a bed of lush vegetation bordering sandy white beaches that stretched as far as the eye could see.

She felt a little apprehensive venturing off the ship into an unfamiliar country alone. She could have signed up for a ship sanctioned tour, but she preferred to do things at her own pace. Besides, she was a big girl. She was used to taking care of herself.

She did a bit of souvenir shopping first, then following the directions from the guidebook she'd purchased at the tourism center, managed to find the Limon Botanical Gardens. René had visited just last year and insisted she make the trip. He said she wouldn't be disappointed, and he was right.

Costa Rica was home to more than three thousand varieties of plant life. She lost herself in the sweet smelling exotic flowers and the feel of thick waxy leaves.

Through an arbor of thick vines and lush ivy, she found herself in a dense rain forest exhibit. It was hot and smelled earthy, like damp moss and soil. Dense foliage lined each side of the narrow dirt path, blocking the sun. It was quiet and dark, and to be honest, a little creepy. She couldn't imagine what it would feel like to be stuck alone in a real rain forest.

She walked slowly, noting the signs identifying each

variety of tree and plant. She touched the leaves, some smooth and waxy, others rough and dry.

When she heard footsteps behind her, she just assumed it was another tourist. She saw only a dark flash of movement in her peripheral vision an instant before a gloved hand clamped down hard over her mouth.

Run! her brain screamed. *Fight for your life.*

She was about to bite down as hard as she could when she felt something rigid and blunt press against her lower back.

A gun, she realized. She stopped her struggle before it had begun.

"Quiet, and you won't be hurt," he said gruffly, in an accent she didn't recognize.

He removed his hand from her mouth and groped around the base of her neck. She stood there frozen, the reality of the situation sinking in. Was he going to choke her? Kill her?

Before fear could sink its claws in very deep, she felt a sharp tug at the back of her neck and heard the snap of the chain that had been hanging there, then she was shoved forward, hard. She landed on her knees in the dirt. But by the time she had gotten her bearings and turned to see if she could catch a glimpse of his face, he was gone.

CHAPTER NINE

CLAIRE SPENT THE rest of the afternoon camped out in the Limon police station. They served her bitter, stale coffee and, despite the fact that she hadn't seen her attacker's face, sat her in an uncomfortable plastic chair at a folding table with a shaky leg to look at mug shots. She studied them until her eyes burned and each face began to look exactly like the one before it. And for all her trouble, she got the equivalent of a pat on the head and was sent on her way.

The police told her she had been lucky to escape the attack with only a few bruises on her neck and scraped knees, but unfortunately the thief would probably never be caught. And for his trouble, all the thief had managed to skulk away with was a cheap silver necklace she'd picked up in a shop in Limon. Wouldn't he be disappointed.

And through it all, the only thing she knew for certain was that she needed to see Liam. Just being near him would make her feel better.

She barely made it back to the ship before it set sail at seven. Though her knees bore the brunt of the fall, her entire body ached, and she was in desperate need of an aspirin. She was still feeling shaky, and she couldn't seem to stop looking behind her.

She pressed the button for the elevator, leaning against the wall for support while she waited. Not only did her body hurt, but her head was beginning to throb from her temples down to the base of her skull.

How would she explain this to Papaw without completely freaking him out? Not to mention that he would kill her when he discovered she'd ventured out alone.

"Claire, there you are!"

His voice was like a salve on her frayed nerves. She turned to see Liam walking her way and a sudden, intense wave of relief swelled up inside her. She had to fight not to run to him and throw herself in his arms.

He wore his usual smile, and the sight of it had tears welling in her eyes.

"You missed rehearsal. I thought—" He stopped in his tracks, taking in her bruised knees and dirty clothing. The smile disappeared from his face. "What happened to you?"

She took a deep breath to steady her voice, so she didn't sound as close to a breakdown as she felt. "I was robbed. But I'm okay."

She could swear the color drained from his face. "Robbed? Where?"

"The rain forest exhibit at the botanical gardens in Limon."

"Limon? Did you take a tour? Was the head of security informed?"

At the risk of yet another lecture on safety, she had to tell him the truth. "I wasn't on a tour. I went alone."

He gave his head a disbelieving shake. "You left the ship to explore a foreign country alone?"

When he said it that way, it did sound like a stupid move. "Yeah."

He took a deep breath and blew it out. He looked itching to ream her one, but he restrained himself. Instead he asked, "Are you okay?"

"A little shaken, and very sore, but it could have been a lot worse." I'm much better now that I'm with you, she wanted to add.

"What was stolen?"

"A cheap necklace."

"The ship's necklace?"

She shook her head. "One I bought in Limon. He didn't even try to get my purse. He just grabbed the necklace and threw me to the ground."

He noticed the bruises on her throat and looked physically pained. Cupping her chin gently, he lifted her face to get a closer look.

After all she had been through, was it completely depraved that his touch was arousing?

"Maybe I should take you to the infirmary."

She turned her face from his hand. "I'm okay, really. Just a few bumps and bruises."

"I should at least take you to security. This should be reported."

That was the last thing she wanted to do. "No, Liam.

Please. I've already spent hours in the police station. I'm exhausted. I just want to go to sleep."

"Please," he said, his tone earnest, his eyes full of concern. "Do it for me."

Well, jeez, when he asked her that way, how could she tell him no?

"Fine. Take me to security."

LIAM WALKED CLAIRE to the security office, a feeling of unease lodged like the ship's anchor in the pit of his stomach. Something about this wasn't right. And as he listened to her tell her story to Sean Brady, the head of security, the sensation grew.

"Because it wasn't a ship sanctioned trip," Sean said, shooting Claire a stern look, "I have no authority. The local police will have to handle it. For the remainder of the trip, however, I suggest you limit your off-ship activities to guided tours."

"I will," she said. "In fact, I doubt I'll leave the ship again until we're safe in Florida. I realize I brought this on myself."

"Claire, could you give us a minute alone? Then I'll walk you to your room."

She nodded. She looked too tired to put up a fight. After she left the office and closed the door, he turned to Sean.

Sean rested his hands against the desktop. "Tell me what's on your mind, Liam."

"Is it only coincidence that this is the third attack on a guest in as many weeks?"

"These things happen from time to time. It's not uncommon for thieves to prey on tourists. Particularly women traveling alone."

"And the sabotage of my show? You don't think this is related?"

"Give me one good reason why I should."

That was the problem. He couldn't. He just had a very bad feeling, and it was rare that his instincts betrayed him. Before he'd boarded the ship, he'd heard of the business with the smuggled artifacts in the Mediterranean segment the previous summer. He couldn't help but feel it might be related somehow.

"I understand your concern," Sean said. "And you'll be happy to know that after what happened this morning in the auditorium, we've increased security. No one is allowed in who isn't directly involved in the show."

"I was under the impression everyone considered that a freak accident. That the grease magically appeared." Liam couldn't keep the sarcasm from his voice.

"How is the dancer who was injured?"

"A few weeks of rest and she'll be fine." But it could have been much worse. Suppose it had been one of the older performers who'd fallen? The end result could just as easily have been a broken hip.

"We're doing everything we can to ensure the safety of both the guests *and* staff. I'm sure we've seen the last of the pranks and mischief."

Deep down, Liam was all but positive they hadn't, but there was no use in pushing the point. Not until he had definitive proof.

He left Sean's office and collected Claire from a chair outside the door. "I'll take you up to your room."

She got up, her movements slow and strained, as though she ached all over. He felt guilty for dragging her here, for wasting her time. He should have let her go straight to bed.

As they were walking to the elevator she asked, "There was another incident?"

He shot her a questioning look.

"Yes," she admitted, "I was eavesdropping. Sean said that someone was hurt this time?"

"Something was spilled on the stage. A dancer slipped and hurt her back."

"That's where you were this morning?"

He nodded, pressing the elevator button.

"And you think my mugging is somehow involved?"

The doors opened and they stepped inside. Liam nodded and smiled to the middle-aged couple standing there. They took in Claire's dirty clothes and bandaged knees with open curiosity.

"Hiking malfunction," she told them.

That earned her an, "Oh you poor thing," from the wife and a sympathetic nod from her spouse.

The bruises on her neck might have been a bit more difficult to explain, but thankfully they didn't seem to notice them.

When they stepped off the elevator at her deck, she picked up right where they'd left off. "So, do you?"

"As I'm sure you heard me tell Sean, I have no reason

to believe your mugging had anything to do with what's happening on the ship."

"Yet you still do. Messing with the set is one thing, but now people are getting hurt. Maybe you *should* put the show on hold."

"That's not my call. Besides, you probably heard him say that he's increasing security."

"But will that be enough?"

For some reason Liam didn't think so. At times he hated these gut feelings he would get, because more often than not he was right. "I guess it will have to be."

They stopped outside her door. "There's something you're not telling me."

"It's difficult to explain."

"Try."

He could see she wasn't likely to let this drop. "It's a bit...*out there.* You probably wouldn't believe me if I told you."

"Are you kidding? I live on an island populated with ex-hippies and New Age freaks. If something is *out there,* I guarantee I've seen it."

"I get these feelings. Impressions. I've had them all of my life."

"So you're psychic?"

He shrugged. "Call it what you will. Psychic powers, second sight, intuition."

She narrowed her eyes at him. "You see dead people?"

Because he knew she was joking, he let that one slide. "I don't actually *see* anything. I only feel."

"And you feel like something else will happen?"

He didn't want to frighten her, but he wouldn't lie, either. "I do. And I'm not often wrong."

The seconds crawled by and Claire just looked at him. Studied his face as though she were searching for…something. "For some reason that I don't understand, or can even explain, I trust you, Liam."

It occurred to him then how deeply attached he had become to Claire, and in such a short time.

He was treading on dangerous ground. He didn't tie himself down to women. Especially women like Claire. She looked tough, acted tough, but on the inside she was all softness and mush. The kind of woman who loved deeply, and crashed hard when a relationship didn't work out. The kind he always avoided.

But this time he couldn't seem to stay away.

"I should let you get to sleep."

"Could you stay just a few more minutes? I have to tell Papaw what happened and he might be a little less angry with me if you're here to run interference."

"Of course." It was the least he could do.

She knocked on her grandfather's door. When he didn't answer she knocked again, louder. "He must be out dancing."

The tough facade slipped a bit. Though she would most likely deny it, he could see that she didn't want to be alone. She needed her grandfather. "I could go find him for you."

"Would you?"

"Of course."

She pulled her card key from her purse and opened her own door. "Thank you for walking me up here."

"My pleasure. Get a good night's rest. You'll feel much better in the morning."

Oddly enough, she looked as though she believed him. What he did next probably wasn't the smartest move, but at that instant he was operating on pure instinct.

He felt himself leaning toward her, saw her chin tip upward in anticipation. His lips barely touching her skin, he brushed a very chaste kiss against her left cheek. Maybe because she looked as though she needed it. Or maybe *he* was the one who had needed it.

Either way, it was the best kiss he'd had in a long time.

LIAM HAD BEEN SO preoccupied with Claire, he had completely forgotten he'd made plans to meet Lily for a drink. He hoped she was still in the lounge waiting for him.

Smooth jazz circa nineteen fifty-something—he was guessing Vince Guaraldi—played softly in the background as he stepped into the piano bar. He scanned the tables and spotted her sitting near the back. He waved to get her attention, then realized her eyes were focused elsewhere. Liam followed her line of vision and saw Claire's grandfather approaching her table.

He yanked his hand down and ducked behind a small group of people chatting by the bar. No way would he interfere when they had made so little progress mending their wounds.

Now he felt grateful he'd been detained.

Lily sat there frozen as Frederick approached. When he spoke, gestured to the empty seat where Liam might have been sitting, she answered him with a stiff nod.

Come on, old girl, don't play hard to get, he thought. Lily could be so stubborn.

Liam realized suddenly that he was supposed to be telling Frederick that Claire needed him. But if Claire knew that they were together, she might not be so hasty to disturb them either.

He watched them for a minute or two. Neither spoke, nor did anyone stomp away in a huff. Baby steps.

Liam felt torn between his loyalty to Lily and his affection for Claire. But there was a simple solution. Rather than play guessing games with himself, why didn't he just ring her room and ask?

He found an unoccupied house phone in a quiet corner of the hotel lobby and dialed her room. She answered after the third ring, her voice soft and sleepy.

"Did I wake you?" he asked, then quickly added, "It's Liam, by the way."

He could swear he felt her smile across the phone line, and it made him smile, too.

"The accent sort of tipped me off. And no, I wasn't asleep. I just got out of the shower."

He could picture her standing beside the phone, swaddled in a towel, her hair wet. Or maybe there was no towel. Maybe she'd been just about to pull on a nightie when the phone rang and stood there wearing nothing at all.

"I'm not naked," she said.

He hadn't spoken out loud, had he? "Why would I think you're naked?"

"Because you're a man, and that's what *all* men think when a woman says she just got out of the shower."

Well, at least he wasn't the only one.

"I just changed into my pj's," she said. "Pink cotton. Not very sexy I'm afraid."

He doubted that. A sack cloth would look sexy on Claire. But he wasn't going to go there. "How are you feeling?"

"Tired and sore and a little loopy."

"Then I won't keep you long. I just thought you might like to know that your grandfather is in the piano bar. I could let him know you need him back in the room. However, he and Lily are sitting at a table together as we speak."

There was a few seconds of silence. "Just him and Lily?"

"Just the two of them."

"Are they talking?"

"Last I saw, they hadn't quite moved past the awkward silence stage."

She was quiet for several seconds, then said, "Don't interfere. The fact they're even sitting together is a pretty big step. Maybe this means they've come around."

"We can hope."

"Not to be presumptuous, but you do plan to spy on them, right?"

"What a ridiculous question. Of course I do."

There was a smile in her voice. "You can give me the dirt tomorrow morning over coffee."

He most certainly could.

"Well, I should let you get some sleep." And since he wasn't going to be having that drink with Lily, he should get changed and make his nightly rounds at the club. Maybe it was time to try the college fraternity look.

"Thanks again for walking me to my room. And for calling me," she said.

"No trouble."

"The honest truth is, I was starting to feel a little lonely. It was good to hear a friendly voice."

"Good night, Claire."

"'Night."

Reluctant to break the connection, he waited until he heard the click at her end, then hung up the phone.

He was letting himself get too close. Everything in his life was quite…temporary. Everything and everyone. He used to keep a flat in London near his parents' home, but his visits had been so rare, there seemed little point. He'd been on the road for so many years, moving from place to place, job to job, back home seemed a million miles away.

He always told himself that someday he would settle and lay down roots. When the time was right.

But what if that time never came?

Despite his feelings for Claire, he didn't want to

give her false hope, the idea that they had any kind of future together.

If this went any further, there was only one way it could end.

Badly.

And if so, why did every instinct he had tell him otherwise?

CHAPTER TEN

LIKE MOST MEN, Frederick wasn't comfortable discussing his feelings. But he'd done a lot of thinking since his conversation with Claire the other night. In fact, Lily was *all* he'd been able to think about. He wasn't sure if he was buying the idea that they might walk away from this as friends, but the least they could do was clear the air. Let the past go where it belonged—in the past.

When he noticed Lily sitting alone in the piano bar, he saw it as a sign. When she saw him approaching her table, her eyes widened and he thought she would turn tail and run the other way.

"May I join you?" he asked.

Her tone was cold as ice. "I'm waiting for someone."

He felt his hackles rise. Waiting for whom? he wanted to ask. Had she met someone? Was this a date?

Was he *jealous?*

What had gotten into him? "Just for a minute," he said.

She considered that for a very long moment, and finally nodded.

He was barely in his chair when the waitress arrived to take his order. He almost told her soda water, but he had the feeling he would need help getting through this conversation, and one drink wasn't going to kill him. "Scotch on the rocks," he said. "And bring the lady another of whatever she's drinking."

"Seven and seven," Lily told her. When the waitress was gone, she asked, "To what do I owe the honor?"

"I figured it was time we talked. Cleared the air."

"Oh you did, did you?"

If he'd expected her to be happy or relieved, he'd been mistaken. "We've been putting this off long enough."

"We?" She folded her arms across her chest. "I recall attempting to talk to you the first day. *You* were the one who wanted nothing to do with me."

"You should have tried harder."

Now she looked mad, and that sure as hell beat the scared mouse look. "Excuse me?"

"The Lily I remember wouldn't have backed down so easily."

"Maybe I'm not the woman I was fifty years ago."

Yes she was. That woman may have been buried deep, but she was still there.

He twisted the knife a little more. "And here I always thought you were the strong one. I'm disappointed in you, Lily."

Her body seemed to snap into place and lock in position. Shoulders high, back straight. She narrowed her eyes at him, making deep creases at the corners. "You think I give a damn how you feel?"

Now, that was the woman he remembered. *His* Lily had finally decided to join the conversation.

He pushed harder. "If you have something to say to me, Lily, then say it. But stop scuttling around with your tail between your legs like a wounded animal."

An angry blush licked its way from the collar of her dress up to her cheeks. "I did have something to say to you. I was going to tell you I made a mistake all those years ago. I loved you, and I never should have listened to my family. I should have forgiven you for what happened. You were only doing what you thought was right. I was going to ask you to forgive me for letting you down. But you know what? I'm too old and life is too damned short for me to be obsessing over this any longer. If you want to let the past go, I would like that, Skip. I would like that a lot. But if this is a grudge you plan to take with you to the hereafter, you go right ahead. I don't care any longer."

A grin spread across his face.

He could see her temper burning hotter, spitting flame and ash.

"What are you smiling at?" she amended.

"I knew you were in there somewhere, Lily. It's good to see you again."

For a moment she didn't seem to know what to say. She just stared at him. Then the hint of a smile flickered across her face. "It's good to be back."

CLAIRE WASN'T SURE WHEN Papaw had made it in last night, so when she left at six fifty-five to meet Liam in the coffee shop, she didn't risk knocking on the door and waking him.

She sure hoped he and Lily had talked things through. And she hoped Liam might have picked up a snippet or two of their conversation. Considering Papaw's recent attitude, Claire would be hard pressed to get any straight answers from him.

When she got to the coffee shop it was packed. Liam was already there, at his usual table. The instant she saw him and he caught her gaze and smiled, she went warm and mushy from the inside out. Oh, man, she was crushing big-time.

She waved and stepped in the line. He motioned her over.

She pointed to the counter. No way would she make it through the morning without caffeine. In turn he held up a cup, pointed to it, then pointed to her. Only then did she notice the second cup on the table.

He'd ordered for her.

It was a simple gesture, so why did she feel so pleased? It wasn't as if he'd bought her a diamond necklace. It was just a simple coffee.

She worked her way through the crowded shop to his table. "Good morning."

He smiled up at her. "Good morning. Have a seat."

She hung her things on the back of the chair and sat down.

He slid one of the cups to her. "Nonfat latte."

"Thank you." She took a sip. "You were so sure that I'd be here?"

He smiled. "You're here, aren't you?"

Yes, she was. And there was nowhere else on the ship she would rather be right now than with him, she realized.

"How are you feeling?" he asked.

"A little sore, but not bad all things considered."

"Have you talked to your grandfather?"

"I wasn't sure when he got in and I didn't want to wake him. He doesn't even know about the mugging yet. I was hoping to catch him at breakfast. How did it go last night?"

"When I checked on them, they were talking. But there was no way for me to get close enough to hear anything that was said."

"Hey, you two!" Tracy appeared beside their table, a gym bag over one shoulder, looking ready for rehearsal. She crouched down beside Claire's chair. "I heard you were mugged yesterday. Are you all right?"

Wow, word sure did spread fast. But it was sweet of her to ask. "Fine. A few bumps and bruises. Nothing major."

"I hope you didn't lose anything valuable."

"Luckily, no. All he got was the necklace I was wearing."

"The ship's necklace?"

"Nope. Just a cheap chain I bought in Costa Rica. I'm beginning to believe the pendant might be good luck after all."

"You're wearing it now?"

Claire reached up to touch her chest where the pendant

usually lay, and remembered that she'd taken it off when she took her shower. "I guess I forgot to slip it on."

"I'm just glad you're okay." She smiled and awkwardly patted Claire's shoulder.

"Can I buy you a coffee?" Claire asked.

"Thanks, but I have to get going." She rose to her feet and hiked her bag over her shoulder. "I'll see you two later."

"She's sweet," Claire said when she was gone.

"She does have her moments," Liam agreed.

Claire shifted in her seat and a hollow ache rolled from her tailbone to the base of her neck. It looked as though it was time for another dose of pain reliever.

She reached around to the back of her chair for her purse but found only her sweater hanging there. Hadn't she brought her purse with her? "Huh."

"What's wrong?"

She turned in her seat and checked underneath the sweater. "That's weird. I could swear I grabbed my purse on the way out of the room. Do you remember seeing it?"

He shrugged. "Sorry, I didn't notice."

"Darn. I must have forgotten it in the room. And of course my card key was in it."

"You can get a replacement at the desk."

She didn't want to ruin the first successful coffee date they had been able to manage, but if she didn't find her purse, it was going to drive her crazy.

He grinned. "You want to go now, don't you?"

It was scary, the way he seemed to read her thoughts. "Is that your second sense at work?"

"More like common sense. I have four older sisters. I remember how traumatic a lost purse can be. Will I see you at rehearsal?"

"I'll definitely be there." The coast guard couldn't keep her away.

SALVATORE WAS TRYING TO get the pendant without her.

It couldn't be coincidence that only two days after Tracy told him who had it, Claire was mugged. How many times had she told him that *she* would get it? If he wasn't careful, he was going to raise suspicions.

She'd overheard Patti and Sean talking this morning. He'd asked Patti if she thought the attacks on the passengers might be related. At this rate, it was only a matter of time before he linked them to the pendant. And that might lead him to suspect the pendant had something to do with the smuggled antiquities. If anyone figured out what was hidden inside, she would never see her little boy again.

She was running out of time.

Clutching her gym bag close to her side, Tracy stepped into the ladies' room. There were two women at the sink washing their hands. They wore matching poodle skirts and saddle shoes. She flashed them both a smile—had to be polite to the passengers—and ducked into a stall.

Please let it be there, she prayed silently. It *had* to be there.

She sat down, unzipped her bag, and pulled Claire's purse out. It was small and light and easy to swipe. Too easy. It was almost frightening how naturally stealing came to her. But this was the last time. Ever. As soon as she had the pendant she was going legit.

She would find a cute little house in a safe neighborhood where she could raise her son. She might even go back to school. Or teach dance, since her days as a professional dancer were limited.

Her hands trembling with excitement and fear, she opened the purse and searched through the two small compartments. Drivers license and credit cards. Lipstick and chewing gum. Seventeen dollars in cash.

But no pendant.

Tracy was overcome by the sudden urge to vomit.

How was this possible? She had *seen* Claire put the necklace in her purse the other day. She hadn't been wearing it the coffee shop.

Could she have lied about it being stolen? Maybe she felt bad because it belonged to *Alexandra's Dream.* But why would she lie about that? As far as she and the rest of ship knew, the pendant was a worthless piece of junk.

She took a deep breath, fought to calm her throbbing heart. It was okay. This was just a small setback. A minor inconvenience. If it wasn't in Claire's purse, or around her neck, the only place left was her room.

No problem. She would wait until Claire joined her grandfather at rehearsal, find some excuse to leave, then sneak into the room with the master key she'd "borrowed" and search for it.

She *had* to find it. If Sal got to the pendant before her, she would have lost her only bargaining chip, and her baby would be lost forever.

IT WAS ODD THAT ONLY a day earlier, Lily and Skip had been strangers—adversaries even—and this morning felt just like old times. Only better. Less volatile. With age, they had also gained wisdom and patience.

"More coffee?" he asked, holding up the carafe.

She patted her mouth with her napkin, hoping she wasn't wiping away her lipstick. At her age, a woman needed all the help she could get. "Yes, please."

He filled her cup, then his own. They had opted to share a private, room service breakfast in her cabin. Just the two of them.

They had stayed up until three a.m. talking. Fifty years was a long time to catch up on and they had barely scratched the surface. She didn't think she would ever run out of things to say to him.

"When you testified at the inquiry, I was so angry I thought I would never forgive you. I didn't understand how you could turn your back on people we considered friends."

"And I was furious with you for throwing your career away. Paying for someone else's poor judgment."

"We were young and idealistic and foolish. Besides, if I'd disobeyed my parents and married you, they would have meddled and picked until they drove us apart."

"It sounds like your marriage to the man they considered Mr. Right didn't work out all that well either."

"He wanted children. I couldn't give him any. I'd suffered through half a dozen miscarriages and a list of female issues a mile long, before I had to have radical surgery. I was still in the hospital recovering when he moved out and filed for divorce."

He shook his head. "How could someone be so cold?"

She shrugged. "Our marriage had never been based on love."

"So you never had children?"

"My second husband and I considered adoption at first, but the marriage didn't last long enough. And in those days a single woman wasn't allowed to adopt. By the time I married my third husband, Liam's uncle Walter, I was considered too old. But we were happy together. We were married eighteen wonderful years when a heart attack stole him from me."

Skip reached across the table and folded his hand over hers. "You've had some sad times."

"And lots of good times, too. You know how it goes."

He nodded. "I love my daughter, but Mira was a handful from the day she was born. We tried being strict, tried loosening the reins. Nothing seemed to work with her. But she gave us Claire."

She turned her hand and gave his a squeeze. "She's very special. I could see that about her right away."

"I worry that she's unhappy. She's had some bad luck with men and I think she's afraid to put herself out there again. Even though she won't admit it, I think she likes Liam."

"I think the feeling is mutual."

He was still holding her hand and it felt nice. Comfortable.

"You should have seen the way those two looked at each other the first time they met," he told her. "I could swear I saw sparks fly. But Claire wouldn't even talk about it."

"Liam either. Maybe all they need is a little nudge."

"What do you mean by a nudge?"

"Since we boarded the ship those two have been nagging you and me to work things out. Right?"

A smile lit his eyes. "What are you up to, Lily-girl?"

She shrugged. "I just think it might be time to give them a taste of their own medicine."

CHAPTER ELEVEN

CLAIRE RUMMAGED THROUGH the contents of her purse a second time to confirm that nothing was missing. "Where did you say they found it?"

"In the ladies' room," the clerk behind the desk in security told her. "It was in one of the stalls."

That was *so* weird. She remembered bringing her purse with her, but had no recollection whatsoever of stopping in the ladies' room. She could swear she had gone straight to the coffee shop. Was she blacking out? Losing chunks of time?

Maybe the mugging yesterday had done more damage than she realized.

"Anything missing?" the clerk asked.

"Looks like everything is here." But she checked again, just to be sure.

When the purse hadn't been in her room she was positive someone had stolen it from the coffee shop. She was on her way out the door to report it to security when they called her to say it had been found.

If someone had stolen it, wouldn't they have at least taken the cash? The credit cards?

But if it wasn't stolen, why couldn't she remember going into the bathroom?

Man, she was losing it.

"Thanks for calling me," she told the clerk.

The clerk smiled. "No problem. Enjoy the rest of your cruise."

Claire left the security office and headed for the auditorium, but as she approached the door, she was stopped by a security officer. A young, cute guy, with biceps to die for. "Staff and cast only, ma'am."

Ma'am?

Ugh. When had she gone from being a *miss* to a *ma'am?* She wasn't *that* old. "My grandfather is one of the performers," she told him. "I need to speak with him."

He didn't budge from his spot in front of the door. "I'm sorry. You'll have to wait until rehearsal is over."

This guy was not getting on her good side. "I've been at almost *every* rehearsal."

"I was given strict orders."

"Ask Liam. He'll tell you it's fine."

"Unless it's an emergency, I can't interrupt. Is this an emergency?"

She couldn't lie to the guy and get everyone in a panic. "Not exactly. But it's important."

"Then I'm sorry. I can't help you."

She tried her pleading face, what Papaw liked to call her gooey eyes. "Just this once? Pretty please?"

He didn't so much as crack a smile. Man, this guy was an ice cube. "You'll have to come back after rehearsal is over."

How would she have handled this in the past? If she were at a club she wanted access into, or a private party she hadn't been invited to, what would she do?

Somehow she doubted that flashing her boobs or offering a cash bribe would carry much weight with this guy.

It would probably just get her arrested.

She checked her watch. Practice would be over in an hour anyway. This would give her time to run back up to the room and freshen up her makeup.

"Thanks for the help," she told the guard, doing her best not to sound snippy and sarcastic.

He nodded. At least he had the decency not to be smug about it.

When she got back to her room, she could hear the phone ringing. She fumbled with her key, flung the door open and dashed for the table. She snatched up the phone and greeted the caller with a breathless, "Hello."

It was Liam. "Where are you? You said you were coming to rehearsal."

"I tried. Your henchman wouldn't let me in."

"Henchman? Oh, you mean Derrick?"

"That guy is about as warm as the polar ice caps. My flirting had absolutely no effect on him."

"Unbelievable. He must be a eunuch."

"He called me ma'am."

"Ma'am?" he said indignantly. "You're not old enough to be a ma'am."

"That's what I thought! Of course, junior looks about sixteen. Maybe to him I look ancient."

"I know where he lives. We could sneak into his quarters and short sheet his bed."

He always had a way of making her smile. "Listen, I've got to get back to rehearsal, but I need to ask, have you spoken with your grandfather yet?"

"Not yet. I planned to talk to him right after rehearsal."

"Neither he nor Lily showed up for rehearsal."

She felt a quick jab of alarm. But before she could work herself into a full-blown panic, she reminded herself that they were at sea on a cruise ship. Odds were they were both fine. "You think something is wrong, or you think they're just playing hooky?"

"Probably hooky, but I want to be sure. I tried ringing Lily's room but there's no answer. I was hoping you could pop by and see if they've stopped there."

"You're just dying to know what happened last night, aren't you?"

He chuckled. "That, too."

Claire jotted down her cabin number. "I'll go right now then I'll meet you outside the auditorium at noon."

"Thanks, Claire. The coffee is on me again tomorrow morning."

Meaning he wanted to have coffee with her again. She liked the idea of Liam being one of the first people she saw before starting her day. She liked the idea of him being the last one, too. The middle wouldn't be bad either.

She hung up the phone before she did something really stupid like admit that he'd gotten under her skin.

Noon couldn't possibly come soon enough.

She knocked on Papaw's door. When he didn't answer, she used her key. The room was empty. She headed to Lily's room next, though she wasn't really expecting to find anyone there. They were probably off having fun together. This was supposed to be a vacation, after all.

Lily's room was around the corner and down the corridor. Claire knocked, waited a minute, then knocked louder, just in case Lily was hard of hearing. She was about to walk away when the door opened and Lily peeked out.

"Yes… Oh, hello, Claire!"

The older woman was wearing a robe and looked as though she had just rolled out of bed. If she was still sleeping, where was Papaw?

Fear lodged in Claire's gut. What if he'd hurt himself? Suppose he fell overboard?

Okay, that was just silly.

"I'm looking for my grandfather. He didn't show up for rehearsal. Have you seen him?"

Lily bit her lip. "Um, yes. I've seen him."

"Recently? Like, this morning?"

She looked uneasy. "Yes."

Were they going to play twenty questions? "Do you know where he is?"

She tugged her robe a bit tighter around her. "Well, yes, I do actually."

Okay. "Can you tell me where?"

"Well…" She glanced over her shoulder, then back at Claire. "Sleeping."

"I was just in his room. He wasn't…" She trailed off.

Lily turned a dozen shades of red.

Oh, Claire. You idiot. He was in *Lily's* room. And Lily was in her robe, which could only mean one thing. "I'm sorry. I didn't mean to interrupt."

"I could wake him—"

"No, no!" That would be *way* too weird. It was one thing to know that he'd loved someone before her grandma. She wasn't ready to deal with him loving someone after her.

"Claire—"

"I'm only here because Liam asked me to come by and check on you." That's good, blame it on Liam. This was his fault after all. "He was worried when you didn't show up. I'll let him know that you're…fine."

She backed away from the door and Lily took a step into the hallway. "Are you angry?"

How could Claire possibly explain to Lily how she was feeling when she wasn't even sure herself? Maybe it was jealousy. She didn't want to think that her grandma had been replaced, that Claire had been pushed into the number two spot in Papaw's heart.

But Lily looked so guilty and embarrassed. What right did Claire have to judge her? To diminish her happiness? As long as Papaw was happy.

She rearranged her mouth into what she hoped resembled a smile. "I want you both to be happy."

"That isn't what I asked."

Lily wasn't going to let this go. "I just need a little

time to let this…" She almost said *fester,* and at the last second threw in, "digest."

Lily nodded. "Fair enough. I'll tell Skip you stopped by."

"Skip?"

"Your grandfather." She laughed lightly. "I guess I'm the only one who ever called him that."

One more thing Claire never would have known about him. "Why?"

"Your grandfather had this tendency to skip his lines. So eventually I started calling him Skip."

Claire would like to hear more about those days. Sometime. Right now it was just too soon. And only after Lily shut the door did Claire realize she still hadn't told Papaw about the mugging.

She had half a notion to knock again, but honestly, the whole mugging ordeal was seeming less and less significant. It had happened, she was fine, end of story. No point in dwelling on it.

JITTERY WITH FRUSTRATION, AND one too many cups of coffee, Tracy watched as Claire met Liam outside the auditorium after rehearsal and the two walked off together. She was so angry with the world, with herself, that she almost wished he would get fired for consorting with a passenger, even though none of this was really his fault.

It wasn't fair.

She had been *so* close. Why had Mr. Miles and Claire picked today to skip rehearsal? It was as if they knew what she had planned and deliberately stood in her way. Taunting her. There was no way Tracy could risk searching Claire's room when she didn't know where they were. If she was caught it would all be over. She would be arrested and she would never see her son again.

What did Claire need with that pendant anyway? Good luck?

Tracy knew that was bullshit. There was no such thing as luck. And if there was she had only the bad kind.

She had four more days. Then it would be too late.

CLAIRE FINALLY CAUGHT UP with Papaw at the afternoon rehearsal. He felt guilt ridden for not being there for her after the mugging, but she assured him that Liam had seen that she was all right, and that seemed to please him. He didn't mention her catching him and Lily in a compromising situation either. And she was grateful, because she wasn't sure she was ready to talk about it.

"Have you heard about the trouble?" he asked her. "The entire cast is talking about it."

Uh-oh. Apparently news had gotten out and made the rounds. Beefing up security was bound to make people suspicious. "What are they saying?"

"Some strange things have been going on. Items missing or damaged. And several people said they've felt as though they were being watched. Now there are people guarding the door."

Claire wondered if anyone was really being watched, or if people's imaginations had gotten the best of them.

"You know something, Claire. Don't you?"

She had promised Liam she would keep what she knew a secret, but it would eventually get out. Wouldn't it? From the hum of concerned voices as the cast assembled, she sensed paranoia had already set in.

Before she had the chance to tell Papaw anything, Liam hopped up onto the stage, his long, lean body hypnotizing her.

"Can I get everyone's attention?"

The room went dead silent, and all eyes snapped in his direction.

"There seem to be some concerns regarding recent events. I won't lie to you. We believe someone is trying to sabotage the show."

The cast exchanged looks of concern and confusion.

"Who would do that?" one of them asked.

"We have no idea who might be responsible, or why."

"Are we in danger?" a woman asked.

"I have been assured by security that the acts of mischief have been stopped. Guards will be posted at the doors twenty-four hours a day."

Uncertainty buzzed from one person to the next.

"I can see that many of you look concerned, and I certainly don't blame you," Liam said. "In all my years in this business, I've never worked with such an elite, gifted group of performers. I feel truly honored to have spent this time with each and every one of you. However, if any of you feel compelled to leave the show, you do it with my and the staff's blessing."

No one said a word, but Claire could see his honesty

had made an impact on them. She wanted to stay, and she wasn't even in the show!

Papaw was the first to step forward and break the silence. "I refuse to quit. I can't imagine why anyone would target a bunch of old-timers, but whatever the reason, we can't let them get the best of us."

Lily stepped up beside him, linking her arm through his. "I'm not quitting either."

One by one the cast nodded in agreement. Tentatively at first. But as more of them stepped up, the group's resolve seemed to grow and strengthen.

Papaw smiled up at Liam. "It looks as though we're all with you, son."

Claire could swear Liam's eyes misted over, and his voice sounded a little rough when he said, "Then let's get started."

He glanced over at Claire and she gave him a thumbs-up sign. He flashed her that adorable grin, and Claire was convinced that if anyone could make this work, Liam could.

Pride and respect overflowed her heart as she watched the cast sing and dance. Rather than dampen their enthusiasm, knowledge of the sabotage seemed to kick-start their spirits into overdrive. Everyone shone like gold dust, but Papaw and Lily—and their incredible onstage chemistry—took Claire's breath away.

She couldn't imagine why anyone would want to hurt these wonderful people, but she could see—and she hoped the person responsible could, too—that they wouldn't let anyone drag them down.

CHAPTER TWELVE

To CELEBRATE THEIR triumph that morning, Papaw made reservations at one of the ship's most exclusive restaurants. Papaw, Claire and Lily shared an exquisite, candlelit meal. At first Claire worried she might feel like a third wheel, but the conversation was lively and the atmosphere enchanting. The food was like magic to the palette, the wine aged to perfection, and the waitstaff treated them like royalty.

She wore her hair up, took the time to apply eyeliner, mascara *and* lipstick. Her cocktail dress was made from a deep emerald satin with a short-waist jacket to match. She accessorized with matching pumps, long white satin gloves, her grandmother's amber costume jewelry, and a small jewel-encrusted purse. She'd even taken the time to set her hair in pin curls and shape it into very authentic looking vintage waves.

All day, before they picked Lily up at her door, Claire feared she might do or say the wrong thing. She and Papaw often reminisced about Grandma, but what if that made Lily uncomfortable? What if Claire gave her the impression she disapproved of their friendship?

Her concerns were dispelled the instant Lily opened her door. When she saw Claire standing there she uttered a soft, breathy gasp. "Claire, your outfit is stunning. You're the spitting image of your grandmother!"

From that moment on the evening only got better. After dinner they shared a decadent chocolate concoction for dessert, then took a moonlit walk on the deck. The only way it could have been better was if Liam had been there.

After she'd spent one evening with Lily, any preconceived notions or concerns Claire may have had evaporated into the warm Caribbean air. For the first time since Grandma had died, Papaw had lost the hint of sadness that seemed to lurk just below the surface. The chemistry he and Lily shared onstage burned even brighter offstage. All night they exchanged secret smiles and held hands.

After one pass around the ship, Claire figured it was time to give the lovebirds a bit of privacy. Despite their protests, she said her good-nights. She gave Papaw a kiss, and after only an instant of hesitation, gave Lily one, too.

"Thank you for dinner," she told them. "I had a wonderful time."

"What do you plan to do now?" Lily asked.

Claire shrugged. "I'm not sure."

"I heard there's a party in that club," Papaw suggested. "Vertigo, I think it's called."

"Yes," Lily said. "Liam mentioned it."

"I'm not really into the club scene," Claire told them.

Papaw turned to Lily. "Isn't part of Liam's job to attend the parties and dance with the ladies? Make sure everyone is having a good time?"

"It is," Lily said. "In fact, I'm sure he's there right now."

Claire looked back and forth between them. "That wasn't half-bad, although you two really need to work on subtlety."

"You should go," Papaw said. "Relax and have fun. Live a little."

The minute they mentioned Liam her choice was made. They didn't have to convince her to go.

She was already there.

IF CLAIRE HAD EVER WONDERED what it would be like to attend a high school dance in the fifties, now she knew.

Colorful balloons, crepe streamers and vinyl 45's lined the walls amidst vintage posters and soc hop decorations. An authentic looking jukebox flashed in the corner and fifties rock and roll blared from the speakers.

Couples in full costume danced the Bunny Hop and the Twist, the Jerk and the Pony, and everyone seemed to be having a blast.

At first glance she didn't see Liam, but the dance floor was packed to capacity. She found an unoccupied table next to the dance floor and sat down. A waitress in a sock hop uniform, complete with roller skates, skidded to a stop beside her.

"Gettcha a drink, hon?" she asked Claire, snapping her gum.

Claire had had wine with dinner and that was usually her limit. Her days of needing alcohol to have fun had ended a long time ago.

"Our specialties are piña coladas, and we have a terrific line of frozen margaritas. Any flavor you want."

Claire felt herself salivating. She *loved* margaritas. Oh, what the heck. Like Papaw said, it was okay to let loose and have fun every once in a while. Besides, how much damage could one or two drinks do? She'd always had an extremely high tolerance for alchohol. In her party days she could drink every single one of her friends under the table. Even the guys.

"How about a watermelon margarita, extra salt."

The waitress snapped her gum and jotted the order on her pad. "That'll be right up, sugar."

The waitress zipped away in the direction of the bar, and Claire turned back to the dance floor, wondering if she could catch a glimpse of Liam. She was curious to see how he would be dressed tonight. Would he choose the bad boy greaser look, or the preppy frat brother?

The waitress returned with her drink in record time. Claire paid what she was guessing had to be slightly higher than a fifties drink price, plus a generous tip.

"Thanks, doll face!" She snapped her gum and skated off.

She sipped her margarita and the sweet, tart flavor exploded like fireworks across her tongue. Oh, that was heavenly. She gazed around the club, craning her neck to see if she could find Liam.

There was a guy in a leather jacket who had a similar build, but dark curly hair. And a blond in a letter sweater, but he wasn't tall enough.

Maybe Liam didn't have to work the dance after all.

Her eyes scanned the crowded room once more, and a man at the bar caught her attention. A soldier, in what looked like an authentic vintage Royal Navy dress uniform. The hat disguised his hair color and he stood with his back to her, but the body type was right.

Finally, he turned, and when his eyes reached hers, the rest of the room, the people and the music seemed to shift out of focus and evaporate like mist. Without breaking eye contact, Liam pushed away from the bar and started walking toward her. The uniform fit as if it had been made for him alone.

Claire had a sudden wild fantasy that Liam was her fiancé, just returned from war, and this was the first time they had seen each other since he had been shipped off for duty. Or better still, they had never met, and this was his last night before he shipped out to parts unknown. It would be love at first sight, instant attraction, and they would have only this night to spend together.

Oh, man, she had seen *way* too many movies.

His eyes still locked on hers, Liam stopped beside her table, tipped his hat, and said, "Ma'am."

She nodded. "Sir."

He embarked on a very slow inspection of her

costume, then shook his head and whistled under his breath. "Claire, you look amazing."

"You're looking rather spiffy yourself. Should I call you soldier?"

He grinned. "Private Bates."

Private was exactly where she wished they were right now.

The upbeat song that had been playing ended, and a slow one began. Liam extended a hand to her. "Would you do me the honor?"

Oh, heck yes, she would. She took a quick gulp of her drink, then slipped her hand in his and let him lead her to the dance floor, where a few dozen couples swayed to the slow, hypnotizing rhythm.

That would be the two of them in only a few short seconds. Liam would be holding her in his arms, closer than they had ever been to each other, and Claire felt as giddy as she did nervous. They both knew they were treading on dangerous ground.

He turned and pulled her to him. His hands came to rest on her waist and hers settled on his shoulders. They were not so close that it might be construed as inappropriate, but near enough that Claire could feel the heat of his body, catch the scent of his aftershave.

He grinned down at her. "That dress brings out the color in your eyes."

"And you look dashing in uniform."

"It was my father's."

"You must be built just like him."

"People have always said we look alike."

Keep up the small talk, she told herself. It might distract her from noticing how good he felt. How perfectly in sync they moved. How she wished she were closer.

"Given the choice, I would dance with only you this evening."

He searched her face. Oh, man, he wasn't making this easy, gazing at her with deep blue, bedroom eyes. Either he wanted her as much as she did him, or he was one hell of a tease. "I'll bet you say that to all the girls."

He shook his head. "Only you."

The song ended far too soon, and he walked her back to her table. "Catch you later, doll."

God, she hoped so.

He winked, tipped his hat, then walked away. Off to seduce another unsuspecting female passenger. She wondered if he had even the slightest clue how sexy he looked, how many women followed him with their eyes.

And he likes me, she told herself.

She sipped her drink and ordered a second, and it wasn't long before someone else asked her to dance. And just as she sat down to rest, another man offered his hand. After that, she barely had more than a moment's rest before she was back out on the dance floor. She danced until she was dizzy, realizing she hadn't had this much fun in years.

Her third drink disappeared and the warm, bittersweet glow of inebriation seeped through her veins. She gave herself permission to enjoy it. And she also gave herself permission to stop before she had too much. Years ago she'd loved to overindulge. She'd liked the feeling of being reckless and out of control.

When she was drunk, she wasn't accountable for her actions. Or at least, that was the way she saw it. The Los Angeles Police Department disagreed. She had lost track of how many times she'd been hauled in for drunk and disorderly behavior. But she was the granddaughter of Frederick Miles, and ultimately all she had ever received was a slap on the wrist.

It was a miracle she hadn't gotten herself into real trouble. When she recalled the times she had driven home with a system full of beer, shooters and wine coolers, it made her cringe.

Even worse were the men she had hooked up with. Sex for the sake of sex, just because she could. Because she needed the validation to feel loved and accepted.

It had taken a long time, and a whole lot of soul searching, but she had learned to love and accept *herself*. And that was never more clear than it was right now.

She was in a club with all the alcohol she could consume, and more than a few men—attractive ones at that—interested in something other than a dance.

But she didn't *need* any of it.

She continued to dance and have fun, but Liam was never far from sight, and every now and then he would catch her eye, flash a secret smile. She watched him dance with other women, hold them and sweep them across the floor the way she wished he could with her. She should have been jealous, because she wanted him all to herself, but instead she felt almost…proud.

Every woman he danced with, young or old, small or large, was showered with the same attention and adoration. When a woman was in his arms, Liam made her feel as if she were the only woman in the world. It may have just been a job, but Liam really cared. And he enjoyed what he did. Enjoyed life.

It had been a long time since she had opened her heart to anyone, since she had met anyone worth the effort. Liam would be worth it.

She supposed some things just weren't meant to be.

When the hour closed in on midnight, Claire decided to step out on the deck for some air and a much needed rest. Only after she'd left the noise and activity of the club did it hit her just how soft around the edges she was feeling.

And that was okay. The important thing was that she knew when to stop.

She walked out onto the deck, gripped the cool metal railing. An endless palette of shimmering, inky blackness stretched out before her. Miles of nothingness, as far as the eye could see.

She felt the weight of the pendant around her neck, reached up to touch it. It felt cool and comforting. Almost…wistful.

If she could make one wish, it would be that Liam were there with her. If the pendant really was good luck, if it had secret, magical powers, would she be standing out here alone?

Then she realized, she wasn't.

CHAPTER THIRTEEN

SHE DIDN'T HEAR HIM, didn't see him, hadn't even caught a whisper of his scent, but Claire instinctively knew the instant Liam walked up behind her. She *felt* him, as real and substantial as the rail under her hands. The decking beneath her feet.

This was too weird.

He leaned against the railing beside her, close, but not quite touching. "Is this a private party?"

"There's always room for one more."

The boat swayed underneath her and she gripped the railing to steady herself. "What are you doing out here?"

"I saw you leave. I wanted to make sure you were okay."

"Fine, just a little tipsy." The ship swayed, and she swayed, and Liam gripped her arm to keep her from toppling over. "Okay, maybe more than just a little. Choppy sailing tonight, huh?"

He grinned, one eyebrow raised higher than the other. "The ship isn't moving, Claire."

"Seriously?"

"Seriously."

Well, damn, that wasn't good.

He gazed down at her, his eyes so blue and honest. All four of them.

Oh, crap, she was seeing double.

Four eyes, two noses, two pairs of lips.

She heard someone snort out a laugh, and realized it had come from her. She slapped a hand over her mouth.

The boat swayed again, or she did, and her face collided with something warm and rough. She opened her eyes to military-green. Liam's jacket, she realized. She was leaning up against him.

How had that happened?

She looked up at him. What would he do if she kissed him right now? Would he push her away, or would he kiss her back? And if he did kiss her back, what would he taste like? How would his lips feel?

Some guys she could look at and just know they were a good kisser. She didn't know if it was the shape of the lips or the curve of the smile, but sometimes she just knew.

Liam had that look.

"You okay?" he asked.

She closed her eyes and nodded, nuzzled her nose into his chest. Breathed him in.

He smelled good. Clean and warm. Fresh, like soap and laundry detergent. And something sexy.

Every fiber of her being told her that she should not get involved with him. Not like this. Unfortunately, that fiber had had as much to drink as she did.

His chest rumbled when he talked, vibrating through her cheek. "Maybe I should get you back to your room."

She propped her chin on his chest and smiled up at him. "Are you going to take advantage of me?"

"Would you like me to?"

She was pretty sure he already knew the answer to that question.

"C'mon," he said, leading her, holding her against his side, one arm looped around her waist.

She could only assume he'd been joking. He wasn't really planning to take advantage of her. Was he?

She tried to remember the last time she had been with a man. The last time one had seen her naked anyway? She'd packed on at least ten pounds since then. Most of it in her butt. And he had a perfectly toned dancer's body. What if he got her naked, looked at her, and thought, *Ack, what have I done?*

That was an easy fix. They would just keep the lights off.

Not that she really believed he was going to take advantage of her. But what if she took advantage of him? What if she made the first move?

Oh, my gosh. Was she actually entertaining the idea of seducing him? Did she want to risk getting him fired?

A voice in her head warned her that she was going to regret this tomorrow.

But all she cared about was right now. And right now she felt too good to care about anything. She was going to enjoy the feeling while it lasted.

CLAIRE LOOKED AMAZING TONIGHT. Feminine and sexy. Liam had had a hell of a time concentrating on the passengers he was being paid to entertain and instead found his attention repeatedly wandering in her direction.

"Would your grandfather be up?" he asked as they stepped off the elevator onto her deck. Someone should see that she got to bed safely. And that someone was not going to be him.

"I doubt it."

Damn.

They stopped in front of her door. "Here we are."

She smiled up at him. A dopey, intoxicated grin. "Here we are."

"Key?" he asked.

She looked blankly up at him. "Key?"

"Unless you plan to sleep in the hallway tonight, we need the key to open the door."

"Oh, right!" She uncoiled herself from his waist, anchored her shoulder to the door frame, and fumbled around in her purse. When she finally found it, she displayed it proudly for him to see. "Got it!"

With uncoordinated fingers, she tried to insert the key into the slot. Upside down.

He grinned and shook his head. "Wrong way, Ace. Flip it over."

"Oooops!" With a giggle, she turned it over and tried again. Now it was backward.

"The little arrow should point to the door," he said, doubting whether she could even see the little arrow. Either that, or she was seeing two or three.

She finally got it turned the right way, but missed the slot by about two inches.

This could take all night.

"Why don't you let me," he said, reaching for it.

She yanked her hand away. "I can do it."

She narrowed her eyes, fighting to concentrate, but kept hitting the pad just below it.

Then she dropped it.

"Ooops!"

Before he could stop her, she dove for it—

And smacked her head on the door frame.

Hard.

"Bloody hell, are you okay?"

She wavered unsteadily for a second and uttered a stunned, *"Ow."*

He tugged gently on her arm, helping her upright.

She clamped a hand over her forehead and looked up at him, tears welling in her eyes from the pain.

Instead she snorted out a laugh. And once she got started, she couldn't seem to stop.

He shook his head. "I'm trapped in a bloody Three Stooges routine."

That only made her laugh harder. She looked down, scanning the floor for the key. "Where did it go?"

"No!" He grabbed her arm to keep her from trying again. Another direct hit and she was going to knock herself unconscious. *"You,* don't move. I'll get it."

She sagged against the door frame, giddy with laughter. He snatched up the key, slipped it in the slot and opened the door, saving them another ten minutes or so of fumbling around.

The room was dark, so he leaned in far enough to switch on the light. "In you go."

He gave her a nudge in the right direction and she stumbled inside. She flung her purse onto the floor and kicked her shoes off. She made it all the way to the foot of the bed before she turned and looked expectantly at him. "Aren't you coming in?"

She obviously expected him to come in. And God knows he wanted to. But that was strictly forbidden. Employees did not go into passengers' rooms unless there was some sort of maintenance involved. He couldn't legitimately classify tucking her into bed as maintenance.

"I'm afraid I can't," he said.

"Why not?"

"Occupational hazard."

She looked confused. "Huh?"

"It's against the rules. I could lose my job."

"That's a dumb rule," she said.

It was in fact a brilliant rule, designed to keep members of the staff like him from making a monumental mistake. "How's your head?"

She let go of her forehead, looking at the palm that had been clamped there. She blinked once, then twice. "Huh."

"What is it?"

She held it up so he could see. "I'm bleeding."

Bugger. She *was* bleeding. "Come here. Let's have a look."

"Nope." She shook her head, knocking herself off balance again. "You've gotta come to me."

"I can't do that."

She shrugged. "Then you don't get to see it. If I bleed to death or slip into a coma, it will be on your conscience."

He doubted either was a possibility. From where he stood, it didn't look that bad. But shouldn't he at least get a closer look? Just to be sure.

That was a sort of maintenance. Wasn't it?

If he were a part of the medical team, maybe. "If it's that bad, perhaps a trip to the infirmary?"

She shook her head. "Nope."

It would be negligent of him not to be sure that she wasn't seriously hurt. And that might open the cruise line up to lawsuits and liability issues. Which would most likely get him fired anyway.

So either way he looked at it, he was potentially screwed.

He glanced in both directions down the hall. No one.

This had disaster written all over it, in at least a dozen languages, but he stepped inside and shut the door.

He walked over to where she stood and she gazed up at him, wearing that goofy smile. He cupped her face in his hands. Her skin was soft and creamy and a faint trail of freckles dotted her nose. He brushed her hair aside with his thumbs. It felt silky against his fingers. She had a lump forming in the middle of her forehead just below her hairline. The area around it was an angry red, but the scratch was minor. So minor in fact that it had already stopped bleeding.

"Well?" she asked. "Am I going to live?"

"Just a bump and a scratch. Although you look as though you've sprouted a horn."

That got him another giggle.

He touched the enflamed area and she winced.

"It hurts."

He tipped her face toward the light and checked her pupils. Same size. Equal dilation.

He was struck again by how extraordinary her eyes were. This close, he could see that the irises weren't a solid shade. More like dots of color. Flecks of green and yellow, and a bit of blue right around the edges.

"Guess I sort of killed the mood," she said.

Thank God for that. "Have you got a bottle of pain reliever?"

She nodded, her head wobbly on her shoulders, like one of those bobble head dolls. "In the bathroom."

"I'll get them. Crawl into bed."

"What about my pajamas?"

"Are you asking for yourself, or me?"

She snorted another giggle.

"Where are they?"

She pointed. "Bathroom."

"Well, then, why don't you go change, and bring the aspirin out with you."

"Good idea. Give me two minutes." She disappeared into the bathroom and the door snapped shut.

If she slept in transparent black lace, he was going to be very upset.

He heard some bumping around, a curse or two, then a flush, and the sound of running water. Then the door opened and out she popped.

He needn't have worried about the black lace. Her

choice in sleepwear was more casual—a pair of baggy bottoms adorned with cartoon bunnies, and a matching T-shirt large enough to swim in with a smiling rabbit that read, *Life. Get One.*

He knew he was in trouble when a woman in shapeless cotton was a major turn-on.

"Bedtime," he said, and led her there by the arm. She flopped down flat on her back on top of the covers, and in the process that too-big shirt rode up, exposing a strip of milky white skin above her waistline. She had a navel piercing, and he could see the edge of a tattoo low on her hip.

There was nothing more arousing than a woman with a tattoo. He also liked the fact she had a little meat on her bones. Soft swells and curves. She looked the way a real woman was supposed to. Too bad he would never have the pleasure of seeing the rest of her.

She sighed and closed her eyes.

"You did take the aspirin, right?"

She opened her eyes and looked up at him. "I forgot."

"Don't go anywhere," he told her and she answered with a limp flop of her hand.

He found a bottle of acetaminophen on the bathroom counter and tapped a couple out into his hand then filled a glass. Next he pulled a washcloth from the towel rack and dampened it with cold water.

Claire was lying exactly as he'd left her. He thought maybe she'd fallen asleep—or passed out—but when he got closer he could see that her eyes were open and fixed on the ceiling.

He took her arm and helped her sit up, then gave her the pills, which she popped in her mouth. He handed her the glass of water. "Drink it all. You don't want to get dehydrated."

She did as he said, then handed the glass back. He set it on the bedside table. "Let's see your head again."

She tipped her face to him. He smoothed her hair back and tucked it behind her ears then wiped away the dried blood with the damp cloth. She winced, but didn't complain.

Being in the position of caretaker, he found it much easier to maintain a level of professionalism.

"You're good at this," she said, watching him.

"I have rowdy nieces and nephews. They're always getting bumps and bruises."

"How many?"

"Five nephews, four nieces, and two more on the way."

"Jeez, is your family Catholic?"

He grinned. "Just large."

He rolled the cloth and pressed it to her forehead. She sighed and closed her eyes. "How large?"

"I'm the youngest of seven."

Her eyes flew open again. "*Seven?* No way."

"It's true."

"Your mom must have been a saint. Or completely insane."

"A bit of both, I think."

"Where are you from exactly?"

"Harlesden, London."

Her brow wrinkled.

"What's wrong?" he asked.

"Why didn't I know that? Why didn't I ask you about your family days ago? Am I really that self-centered?"

"Not self-centered. It's a self-defense mechanism."

"You think so?"

Liam nodded. "If you don't get to know people, you don't get attached. It's hard to get hurt if you keep people at arms length."

"You sound as if you know a lot about that."

"I'm as closed off as they come."

"But you're so friendly and outgoing," she objected.

"Yet you know nothing about me. Funny, isn't it?"

"If you want to know about me, all you have to do is look in the gossip rag archives."

"That's only the way other people perceive you. Not who you really are."

"So, who are you?"

A man who had to get the hell out before he revealed too much. He removed the cloth from her forehead and draped it over the empty glass. "I'm going to go now."

She grabbed his wrist. "Don't. Don't leave."

"I have to."

"Tell me more about your family."

He hesitated. He needed to go, before this got too cozy. He would use the excuse of work, but it was past midnight and he was officially off duty.

"Claire…"

"Please." Her eyes seemed to plead with him and she said softly, "I want to know who you really are."

CHAPTER FOURTEEN

LIAM WOULD NEVER HAVE imagined Claire could look so fragile or vulnerable, and like a snowball left in the sun, his heart melted into a pile of mush, right along with his spine.

He just couldn't make himself tell her no.

He didn't *want* to leave. He wanted to know her. For her to know him.

"I'll stay for a bit. Lie down."

"I feel less spinny when I sit up." She propped the pillow on the headboard and leaned back against it. "What do your parents do for a living?" she asked.

If he was going to stay awhile, he might as well get comfortable. He pulled off his jacket and draped it across the foot of the bed. "My dad was an English literature professor. My mum was a nurse. They're both retired now. What about your mum and dad?"

"Mira acted occasionally, milking the Miles name for all it was worth. My dad was a *musician*." She made quotation marks with her fingers. "But mostly they just took drugs and acted irresponsibly."

"You resent them."

She shrugged. "The truth is, it sounds worse than it really was. Not that I wasn't completely screwed up. But I think that was more genetics than environment. When two screwed up people breed, you get screwed up kids. But everyone has issues, and I dealt with it."

"That's an interesting way to look at it." He propped one hand on the mattress beside her leg. "You sure you're not giving genetics more credit than it deserves?"

"I had it good as a kid. My grandparents took care of me when my mother bailed out. We had money. Nothing to complain about. I was rebellious by nature." Her hand came to rest over his. It wasn't a sexual overture, more like a friendly gesture. "You're not, though. I'll bet you did everything your parents told you."

"I've always been more of a go with the flow kind of guy. But I had to be. By the time I came along, I think my parents were a bit burned-out."

"Is that the politically correct way to say you were ignored?"

"When I needed attention, I found ways to get it."

She sat up a bit, looking interested. "What did you do?"

"Probably not what you're thinking. Nothing deserving a smack on the bum. Say for example we were at supper. It was next to impossible to get a word in edgewise, so out of the blue I would sing show tunes at the top of my lungs. That usually did the trick."

She laughed, absently tracing the back of his hand with her thumb nail. Intimate, but not deliberate. That knowledge did little to stop him from becoming aroused.

"You know, I hardly ever drink anymore and I haven't been out dancing in forever," she said. "I've been on my best behavior for so long. Maybe tonight I just needed to blow off steam."

"It's tough repressing what's inside you."

"You have no idea." Her hand was on his wrist now, her fingers lightly stroking, back and forth. He watched, mesmerized.

When he looked up, their gazes collided and locked.

She leaned in slightly and her other hand came to rest on his thigh, just above his knee.

"Claire, what are you doing?"

She flashed him a smile steeped in suggestion. "Trying to get your attention. The thing is, I have a lousy singing voice, so the show tunes thing wouldn't work."

Well, her method had worked. In fact, every part of his body had risen to full attention.

She gazed up at him, her eyes innocent and seductive at the same time. "If you kissed me right now, I wouldn't stop you."

Bloody hell.

He wanted to. God knows he did. But this relationship was a dead end. To sleep with her then let her go would only lump him in with the rest of the men who had let her down. He was guessing the list was long enough already.

Claire intrigued him, but he didn't have time for a

relationship. It was more than he was willing to give right now. And she deserved better.

"And then what?" he said. "We sleep together?"

Her eyes didn't stray from his, not even for a second. He didn't even see her blink. "I know what I want, Liam."

He didn't doubt that. But that wasn't the point. Recognizing a mistake was useless if you did nothing to prevent it. "I'm not going to kiss you."

"What if I kiss you?" she asked.

Please don't, he wanted to say. Their attraction was too intense. It would be so good, so perfect, they would both want more. They would take and take, but at some point she would want more than he was capable of giving.

She lifted her hand from his leg, let go of his wrist. Thank God. He closed his eyes, breathed a quiet sigh of relief…and sucked it back in when he felt her touch his face.

Bloody hell, she was making it difficult for him to do the right thing.

He kept his eyes closed, thinking that if he didn't look, didn't see her, it would be possible to walk away.

Wrong.

He felt glued to the bed. Frozen in place. He felt the heat of her body when she moved closer, the softness of her hair brush against his cheek. She smelled sweet and spicy at the same time. Apples and cinnamon. And sex.

She was determined, meaning this couldn't possibly

be considered his fault, right? She knew what she wanted. She'd said it herself.

That is total bollocks, Liam, and you know it.

She was intoxicated. That alone was reason enough to put an end to this now. He felt her breath on his lips, warm and damp.

He bit back a groan, curled his fists into the duvet.

Her arms slipped around his neck, pulling him down. Then her lips brushed his, so sweet...

Then it was over. Over before it began.

He opened his eyes and she smiled up at him. "Was that really so awful?"

Quite the opposite in fact. And though he would never have imagined kissing her so chastely would be enough to pacify his insatiable curiosity, somehow it was. Despite how much he wanted her, simply talking was all he really needed.

He unbuttoned his cuffs, untucked his shirt, and made himself comfortable beside her. "Why don't you tell me more about your mum."

CLAIRE WOKE SLOWLY TO A hammering behind her temples.

Then she remembered last night, and smiled. She and Liam sat for hours talking. In fact, she had never told anyone so much about herself in so short a time. And she knew so much about him. That his favorite color was blue and his family physician when he was growing up was Doctor Fear.

Silly meaningless details that, tied together, formed

something solid and secure. They talked so long, she didn't remember him leaving.

She rolled onto her side and collided with an unyielding bump. Her eyes still closed, she gave the bump a poke.

It grumbled.

She opened her eyes and blinked to clear the sleep from them, then blinked again to be sure she was really seeing what she thought she was seeing.

She couldn't remember Liam leaving, because apparently he'd never left.

He was on his side facing her, long pale lashes resting against his cheeks. For several minutes she watched him, knowing this might be the only time she saw him this way, and she wanted to remember every detail. Every line in his face, each pale freckle.

But he was going to have to report for duty.

She gave his shoulder a gentle nudge. He grumbled. She did it again. "Liam, wake up."

He opened one eye and smiled. "Hey there."

"We fell asleep."

His eye slipped closed. "Hmmm."

She propped herself up on one elbow. "Don't you have to work?"

"Not till morning," he mumbled.

"I hate to break it to you, but it is morning."

She had never seen anyone move so fast in her life. One second he was out cold, the next he was upright and wide awake. "*Bloody hell,* what time is it?"

She looked over at the clock. "Six a.m."

He cursed and rolled out of bed, simultaneously tucking in his shirt and shoving his feet into his shoes.

"I doubt there are very many guests up and around this early."

"It's the staff I'm worried about." He fumbled with his cuffs, and when the buttons wouldn't cooperate, he rolled them instead. "They will be up. And won't it be fun trying to explain why, at six a.m., I'm still wearing the clothes from the night before. And what shall I tell my bunk mate when he asks where I was all night?"

She hadn't really thought of it like that. She pushed herself upright and sat cross-legged. "I'm so sorry. This is totally my fault. I made you stay."

He stopped adjusting his clothing and took a deep breath. "Claire, this is not your fault. I'm here because I wanted to be. I shouldn't have let myself fall asleep."

"It was nice though. Talking to you."

"And it's not often I go to bed with a woman I'm madly infatuated with and wake in the morning with my clothes still on."

"Me neither," she said, then swiftly added, "But in my case a man."

"Damn, and here I was working up quite a fantasy." He grabbed his jacket. "I don't think I'll make coffee this morning."

"That's okay. If I drank coffee right now I would probably yak."

He leaned over and pressed a quick kiss to the top of her head, then headed for the door.

"Hey, Liam!"

With his hand on the knob, he stopped and turned back to her.

"The other day, when you said we would fall in love. Was that just a clever device for scaring me off, or was it one of your psychic impressions?"

For a second he just looked at her, then he said, "Too much knowledge can be a frightening thing."

Then he was gone.

So he'd felt it, too. And the only way to prevent disaster was not to fall in love in the first place.

Only, in her case, it was already too late.

CLAIRE DESPERATELY WANTED TO crawl back into bed and sleep off her hangover, but she had promised Papaw they would have breakfast together. Just the two of them.

When he knocked at seven-fifteen, she was showered and dressed and resembled something vaguely human.

He took one look at her and frowned.

"Yes, I drank too much."

He eyed her sternly. "We're drinking again, Claire?"

"You're the who told me to have fun."

He just looked at her.

"Besides, you have nothing to worry about," she said, rubbing the dull ache at her temples. "The after part is a lot worse than I remember."

She let him in and shut the door. "The room service menu is on the desk by the phone. Order whatever you want. I probably won't be eating much."

"The funniest thing happened last night," he said as

he walked to the desk. "I woke up around two and I could swear I heard voices coming from your room."

"Voices?"

He picked up the menu and flipped through it. "A man and a woman's."

Darned hearing aids. He could hear a cat walk across the carpet. And he didn't even have a cat. "Oh, I must have fallen asleep with the television on."

Yes! Nice save, Claire.

"That's funny. I heard the same thing this morning when I got up."

She couldn't tell if he was fishing, or he knew exactly what he'd heard. "I guess the television was still on."

"I heard your door close, and thinking you might have forgotten our date, I peeked into the hall."

Uh-oh.

"I saw a fellow who looked just like Liam walking to the elevator." He finally set the menu down. "Know anything about that?"

Looked like it was time to fess up. "I was tipsy, so Liam walked me to the room, but I hit my head—" she showed him the small nodule on her forehead "—and I more or less guilted him into coming inside to see if I was okay. Long story short, we got to talking then fell asleep. Nothing inappropriate happened. Except I did kiss him, but it was a really little kiss."

"And?"

She blew out a breath and collapsed onto the love seat. "And I think I'm falling in love with him. But I can't fall in love with him."

He walked over and sat on the cushion beside her. "Sometimes, sweetheart, God doesn't give us a choice. When you meet the right one, you just know. Now, let's see that bump."

He inspected her head, much the way Liam had. They were a lot alike, Liam and Papaw. She'd heard it said that women married their fathers, and Papaw was the only real father figure she'd ever had. Maybe that was why Claire was so drawn to Liam.

Not that she really thought she would ever marry him.

Her grandfather pressed a gentle kiss to her forehead, cupped her face in his hands and just looked at her.

What would she do when she lost him? Who would she have then? Mira? Her absentee dad?

When Papaw was gone, she would truly be alone.

"Are you disappointed in me?" she asked.

"Claire, I'm *proud* of you. I know that what you did last night couldn't have been easy."

"But we didn't *do* anything."

"You talked. You connected. The other part, the physical part, that's easy."

She shrugged. "Not that it matters. We have no future."

"Why do you say that?"

"I live in Canada, he lives on the ship. And the last thing I want is a long distance relationship. Not to mention that he's not exactly the settling down type."

"Like I said, when the right one comes along, you know it."

Maybe Papaw had a point. Maybe Liam was her right one.

But was she his?

LIAM HAD HOPED CLAIRE would come to the coffee shop that evening. It had been a long, busy day and he still had things to do before he went off duty. But more important was spending a few minutes with Claire. He'd bought her a latte just in case.

When he saw her walk in, when she looked over at him and smiled, every rotten detail of his day evaporated.

He stood to greet her, and offered a chair. "I trust you're feeling better."

"A little." As she sat down, he caught the subtle scent of cinnamon. The tips of her hair brushed across his fingers. And damned if he didn't feel those first twinges of arousal. "I think my days of irresponsible alcohol consumption are officially over."

He slid her coffee to her.

"Thank you." She stared at her cup, running her thumb nail up and down one side. "While we have some time alone, I was hoping we could talk."

"We are talking."

She shot him a look.

"Oh, *that* kind of talking," he said. So much for the ignore-it-and-it-will-go-away theory. He should have realized that wasn't Claire's style.

It wasn't really his either.

"I feel like a complete idiot," she said, getting right to the point. He liked that about her. She wasn't afraid to put herself out there and say exactly what was on her mind. With Claire, he never had to play guessing games.

She was unlike any woman he'd ever known. Although he hadn't yet decided if that was a good or a bad thing. Or a bit of both.

"Why would you feel like an idiot?" he asked.

"I pretty much forced you into my room."

"I told you this morning, I was there because I wanted to be."

She gazed up at him through strawberry lashes and the look of vulnerability in her eyes nearly melted him. "Did anyone find out?"

"Patti did. When I told her."

Her eyes widened. "You told her?"

"Better she hear it from me now than in a day or two when everything is twisted and misconstrued."

"What did you tell her?"

"The truth."

If Claire's eyes stretched any wider they would fall from the sockets. *"Everything?"*

He grinned. "Not quite everything."

"What happened?"

"I've been given a formal warning. If it happens again, I'm sacked."

"Then you might not like what I have to say."

That didn't sound promising. "Let's hear it."

"I'm not good at this sort of thing, so if it comes out weird, I apologize." She stopped and took a deep breath. "I've been doing a lot of thinking, and I think you were right."

"About?"

"Our feelings for each other. Because I've got some

really strong feelings for you. And I think maybe you have the same feelings for me."

"I think you said that quite well." It was a lame acknowledgment, but under the circumstances the best he could manage. Telling her they would fall in love before the fact was one thing. Actually admitting he was right was a bit more difficult.

"But we both know this could never be anything but temporary. Wednesday is the end of the line."

He knew what was coming next. She was going to suggest that for the remainder of the cruise, they not see each other.

She leaned closer and lowered her voice. "That's why I think we should sleep together."

He opened his mouth to speak, but he didn't have the faintest clue what to say. Finally he managed a puzzled, "Excuse me?"

"We feel the way we feel. There's no preventing that now. So shouldn't we take advantage of the time we have together?"

"Claire, you do realize that's a *guy's* line."

"You're hiding behind humor."

Of course he was. That was what he did. And with anyone else it probably would have worked. But Claire wasn't just anyone. He leaned forward and said quietly, "You deserve better than a fling. You know that."

Anger sparked in her eyes, and she leaned forward and said in a haughty whisper, "Why does everyone think they know what's best for me? Who the hell are you to tell me what I deserve? Maybe I deserve to get laid, you ever consider that? Maybe I just want sex."

He leaned forward, keeping his voice low. "That's the problem, isn't it? You and I both know that it wouldn't be *just sex*."

She sat back, looking stunned. And for the longest time she said nothing.

He had rendered her speechless. Had he not seen it with his own eyes he never would have believed it.

"I won't do that to you, Claire. I won't be that man. I care too much."

For a very long moment neither said a word. It was clear they had said all there was to say on the matter. So why did he have the feeling that nothing had been resolved?

CHAPTER FIFTEEN

"THIS IS BECAUSE of the show," Claire said to Sean, and Frederick knew she was right.

They had returned from an afternoon workshop to teach youngsters on board the basics of method acting, only to find Claire's room ransacked. Clothes had been ripped from the drawers, her suitcases searched. Toiletries had been dumped to the bathroom floor and smashed.

The most disturbing part was that there was no forced entry. Whoever had done this used a key to get in.

"You're sure nothing is missing?" Sean asked.

"Nothing," Claire said.

"Maybe it was only supposed to look like a robbery," Lily suggested. "To scare you away."

"Well then, it didn't work." Claire bent over and scooped clothes off the floor. "I'm not scared. I'm ticked off."

"It's not just you," Sean admitted. "Several other cast members have received warnings today."

"What kind of warnings?" Lily asked.

"Notes under the door. No specific threats. More of a *quit or else* message."

Lily looked concerned. Frederick hated to see her upset. This cruise was supposed to be fun. Why would someone try to ruin that?

"So are they quitting?" Lily asked.

"Not to my knowledge," Sean told her.

"I'm not quitting either," Frederick said.

Lily slipped an arm around his waist. "Me either."

"In fact, we have to get to rehearsal," he said firmly, and for once no one argued with him. It was going to take a lot more than a ransacked room to scare him away. "Are you coming with us, Claire?"

"I'll stay back and clean up first. I'll try to be there by four."

"Do you need anything else from us?" he asked Sean, in a tone that suggested the answer had better be no.

"If I do, sir, I'll find you."

He hooked his arm through Lily's and led her out of the room.

"You sure told him," she said as they walked to the elevator.

"It's not in my nature to be rude, but sometimes I get sick of people treating me like an old man."

"It's strange, isn't it, how differently people look at you as you grow older?"

Not him. In his eyes, Lily was still the spunky, tough girl who never let anyone knock her down. No matter how old either of them lived to be, that would never change.

The chemistry they'd had all those years ago, the

magic on-screen and off, was still there. He'd never believed he could love a woman as much as he loved Marie, and if he did, he thought it would diminish the importance of his marriage. He could see now that was ridiculous. Marie and Lily were as different as night and day. He could never compare them. And he could never love one more than the other.

"You do realize we're half an hour early," Lily said.

"I guess I just needed to get out of there."

She shrugged. "So we'll dance alone for a while."

"What about music?"

She smiled and squeezed his arm. "We'll make our own music."

When they entered the auditorium, Tracy was already there. "Hey, you two are early. Is everything okay?"

He wondered if maybe she had caught wind of the threats. "We just thought we might get a little extra practice in."

She looked relieved. "Great! Let's get started!"

They began with the second number, and it was clear after a very short time that the private lessons had paid off.

"Wow. You guys are awesome!" Tracy gushed, as he pulled off a dance step that a few days ago had had him tripping over his feet.

"It's my partner," Frederick said, making Lily smile. After all these years she still had the prettiest smile he'd ever seen. "She's so good, she gives the illusion that I am, too."

Lily giggled like a schoolgirl. "Don't listen to him, Tracy. He taught me everything I know."

Years ago she used to say that to make him feel good, but Lily had studied dance and voice since she was old enough to balance on two feet. He found it ironic that her mother had encouraged her to be the best, the most accomplished in her private school, yet when Lily wanted to use that talent and make a career for herself, it had been considered inappropriate.

But the past was the past. There was no sense concerning themselves with what might have been. They were together now and that was all that mattered.

He spun Lily and dipped her, heard an odd creaking noise. Thinking it was his tired old bones, he braced for a wave of pain. But it never came.

He looked down at Lily to find that her mouth had formed a perfect O shape, and her eyes had widened with alarm.

Had it been her bones he'd heard creaking? Had he hurt her? Then he heard a scream, and felt a ghostly presence shoving him forward.

They were falling, he and Lily. It seemed to happen in slow motion. He tried to lean to the left, to hit the floor beside her for fear that he might crush her. But Lily grabbed hold of his shirt lapel and yanked so hard to pull him closer he heard the fabric rip in her hands.

Something exploded and he landed with a heavy thud amid a shower of shattered glass. It shook the floor beneath them and rattled his eardrums.

Then there was just pain.

IT TOOK CLAIRE LESS than twenty minutes to straighten up the room, then she went to the store to replace the toiletries. It was after four when she got to the auditorium. As she rounded the corner she was startled to see the entire cast waiting outside in the lobby. What the—?

Practice should have begun ten minutes ago. Had there been another prank?

She scanned the crowd, realizing immediately that it wasn't the entire cast.

Papaw and Lily were missing.

Eleanor noticed her standing there and rushed toward her. The look on her face stopped Claire cold.

Something had happened. Something bad.

Papaw.

Her heart slithered down to the tips of her toes.

"Oh, honey!" Eleanor gushed, darting toward her. "Everyone has been looking for you! Where have you been?"

Her tone suggested that whatever had happened, Claire's not being there on time was somehow to blame.

She shouldn't have stayed behind to clean the room. She should have been with him. This was all her fault.

"What happened?" Claire asked, but her voice sounded empty and hollow, as if she were in a tunnel.

Eleanor wrapped one chubby hand so tightly around Claire's wrist it stung, and dragged her toward the auditorium door. "Comin' through!" she hollered, her body acting as a battering ram through the crowd, like Moses parting the Red Sea. Claire trailed dutifully behind, too dazed to do much else.

This wasn't happening. It had to be a dream.

The security officer stationed at the auditorium door stopped them. "I'm sorry. No one is allowed inside."

"It's all right," she heard someone say, and turned to see the iceman standing there. "She's the granddaughter."

The other guard nodded. "She can go in."

The guard pushed the door open and Claire saw a group of people both on and off the stage. Most of them were wearing cruise line uniforms. A sea of crisply pressed white. Her heart throbbed in her chest, a sickening thud, then she saw Lily standing near the stage. She looked pale and rumpled but okay. Beside her stood Liam.

When they saw Claire, the look on their faces made her knees go weak.

Where was Papaw? Why couldn't she see him?

She felt a hand on her arm and realized that she must have swayed because the iceman was holding her steady.

"You okay, ma'am?" His voice sounded garbled and faint.

Then Liam was sprinting down the center aisle toward her. She realized then that she wanted nothing more than to collapse in his arms. She wanted him to hold her and stroke her hair and tell her everything would be okay.

It seemed to take him hours to close the distance between them. He took the opposite arm, his hand cold against her skin.

She felt cold all over.

"I've got it from here," he told the guards, then he was leading her into the auditorium. Pulling really, because her feet didn't seem to want to move.

She wanted to know. But she didn't want to know. Then she realized Liam was talking to her, but his words sounded jumbled and nonsensical. She caught a few phrases, things like "minor bumps and scrapes" and "could have been much worse," but she wasn't sure if she was actually hearing him, or hearing what she wanted to hear.

The crowd of people in front of the stage parted and she saw Papaw sitting there. When he saw her and Liam walking toward him, he smiled and waved.

Relief crashed down over her like a tidal wave and for a second she couldn't draw in a breath.

He wasn't dead. He was okay.

Only then did she realize that her hand was at her throat, clutching the pendant. Her good luck charm. Once again it had done its job. It had kept her and her loved ones safe.

As she drew closer to the stage she could see that Papaw's left forearm was bandaged.

"What happened?" she asked Liam.

He shot her a confused look. "You didn't hear a word I just said, did you?"

She shook her head, and the motion seemed to work loose the last of the fog in her brain. She could see and hear everything now, with startling, Technicolor clarity.

She must have looked awful, because the first thing out of Papaw's mouth, as she wrapped her arms around his neck and held him, was, "I'm all right, sweetheart. I'm okay."

She squeezed him tight, pressing her cheek to his chest, feeling his solid warmth, the steady thump of his heart beating strong. "What happened?"

"He just missed being clobbered by a falling stage light," Liam said.

She held Papaw at arm's length and looked at Liam. *"What?"*

He gestured to the stage and she finally noticed the enormous light fixture and shattered bulbs lying there.

"How did this happen?"

Liam and Papaw looked at each other, and she knew there was something they didn't want to tell her. And she knew deep down in her gut that this hadn't been an accident. "Someone did this on purpose," she said.

"We don't know for sure. Someone could have tampered with the light, or it's possible it was never installed properly."

"You don't really believe that."

"We have someone up there inspecting every screw and bolt. No one will be allowed back in until it's deemed safe."

Claire realized, as rumpled as Lily appeared, she must have been involved as well. "Are you okay?"

Lily smiled. "Fine, honey. Just a few scrapes and bumps."

"She saved my life," Papaw said. He smiled and

patted Lily's cheek. "If she hadn't pulled me out of the way it would have crashed down right on top of me."

The realization of just how close she'd come to losing him hit Claire square in the chest. It forced the air from her lungs, and her hands began to tremble.

"Something has to be done," she told Liam, her voice as shaky as her hands. In fact, she was shaking all over.

"Guards will be posted by the door 24-7. No one will be able to get in."

Tears stung her eyes. "For all the good it's done so far!"

"We have no idea when this happened. It could have been days ago, before security became involved. Or months even."

She couldn't believe what she was hearing. "So what you're saying is, you're still doing the show. What do they have to do to get their point across? *Blow up the ship?*"

"Claire," Papaw said firmly, and she realized everyone had stopped what they were doing to stare at her. "Calm down."

Instead she felt an almost irrational need to scream at the top her lungs until someone put an end to this.

"Nothing has been decided yet," Papaw said. "The cast will meet tomorrow morning with Liam, Patti and Sean to discuss the situation."

Claire was so wired her teeth had begun to chatter. Was this what it felt like to be in shock, or was she having a nervous breakdown? This was supposed to be a relaxing vacation, but the way things were going, they would have to drag her off the ship in a straitjacket.

Papaw put a hand on her shoulder. "You need to calm down."

No kidding.

"Maybe you should lie down awhile before dinner," he said.

Dinner? The lump in her throat had grown so enormous she felt as though she would never be able to eat again. But she nodded. If she was going to have a total emotional meltdown she didn't want to do it in front of the entire security staff. They might lock her in the padded room. If the ship even had one.

"Liam, could you see that she makes it up to her room?" Papaw said. "And would you mind terribly staying with her for a while? They need me down here and I don't think she should be alone."

"I would be happy to," Liam told him.

Claire didn't bother to tell Papaw that Liam wasn't allowed in her room. But maybe there were exceptions in a situation like this.

"I'll be up later," Papaw said, giving her a hug. She clung to him, wishing she never had to let go. "Try to get some rest."

She wasn't sure her voice would work, so she nodded and reluctantly let her arms drop. Liam took her by the elbow and led her out of the auditorium. Most of the cast had gone. Only a few stragglers remained and were speaking to Patti.

Everyone turned to look at her and Liam.

"I'm taking Ms. Mackenzie up to her room," Liam told Patti. "Her grandfather asked that I stay with her for a bit."

It was as much a question as a statement. And Claire must have looked pretty bad, because despite what had happened the other night, Patti nodded and told Liam, "Take your time."

Liam walked her to the elevator and they rode up in silence. She kept waiting for him to say something, to shower her with words of comfort. But he didn't seem to have any left. He just stood there, his jaw tight, eyes forward.

He was upset with her, she realized. For causing a scene. For losing her cool and probably making him look bad in front of everyone.

The only thing worse than his anger was knowing she had disappointed him. And the only reason she would care that she disappointed him was if she loved him.

So it was official.

When they got to her room she didn't even bother trying to get the door open. She handed the key to Liam and he opened it for her. She didn't have to coax him in this time. He followed her inside and closed the door, probably eager to give her what for.

She closed her eyes and swallowed hard to keep from crying, bracing herself for whatever might come next. Knowing that whatever it was, she probably deserved it.

And the next thing she knew, she was in his arms.

CHAPTER SIXTEEN

LIAM DREW CLAIRE TIGHTLY against him and she was so surprised that for a second she forgot to breathe.

He never ceased to amaze her. And baffle her.

Before he could change his mind and decide he was mad at her after all, she wound her arms around him and buried her face against his shirt. He stroked her hair, her back, his body warm and solid. And gradually, she began to feel better.

It was scary, the way he always knew just what to do. She had known him seven days, and somehow it felt like a lifetime. And he was right. This was so much more than physical attraction. She wanted Liam in every way possible.

It was wonderful and terrible, because no matter what happened now she was going to get hurt. It was a done deal.

It was simply a matter of when.

She lifted her face and looked up at him. Their eyes locked and something passed between them. Some sort of understanding. He knew what she wanted, what they both *needed*, and this time he wasn't going to fight it.

Maybe it had been inevitable.

She rose up on her toes the exact instant he lowered his head, and when their lips touched, warm and soft and sweet, it took her breath away. It was more perfect, more amazing than she could have possibly imagined.

He pulled back and looked at her, his lids heavy. "You're sure this is what you want?"

Everything inside her said this was right, said he was the one, and she was tired of second-guessing herself.

"I am so completely sure." She snapped the dead bolt into place and walked backward toward the bed, tugging him along with her.

"You're shaking."

He was right. Her hands were trembling and her heart was beating so hard she could feel it in her throat.

"Are you sure?" he asked again.

"I'm sure. Honestly. It just feels like we've been working up to this for a long time. And now that we're actually here, I want everything to be perfect. I don't want you to be disappointed."

He grinned down at her. "That would be impossible. You've already exceeded my expectations."

That's because he hadn't seen her naked yet.

But not for long. He unfastened the buttons on her shirt.

One at a time.

Veeery slowly.

His eyes on her face.

When he was done, he slipped the shirt from her

shoulders and let it fall to the floor. Then he stopped and just looked at her.

So much for her genius plan of having the lights off. It was four-thirty in the afternoon. But he seemed to like what he saw.

She tugged his shirt from the waist of his pants and he pulled it over his head.

Wow.

His arms and chest, his shoulders were better than she had imagined. He was beautiful. Perfect.

He reached for the snap on her shorts and she cringed. "What's wrong?"

"How would you feel about getting undressed under the covers?"

He popped the snap. "Absolutely not."

"I have a big butt," she said, just in case he hadn't noticed. She didn't want him to be too shocked and horrified when he saw it for the first time.

He unzipped her shorts and pushed them down, then stood there *looking* at her again. Caressing her skin without even touching it.

Did he have to do that?

He unfastened his belt and undid his pants. She watched, transfixed, as he took them off. Boxers and all.

He was beautiful and perfect, and she couldn't tear her eyes away. He reached behind her to unfasten her bra. He attempted it with one hand first, and when that didn't work, used both. But after a minute of twisting and tugging he began to get exasperated. "Is this thing padlocked?"

For some stupid reason his lack of finesse was a comfort.

She reached back and unfastened it for him, and with no hesitation tossed it to the floor with the rest of the clothes. In this area she was confident. As far as breasts went, hers were above average. And considering the look on his face, he wouldn't be complaining.

He reached up and touched the tip of one, just a light brush of his fingers, and she shivered.

"Time to lose the panties, Claire."

Oh, man, she really hated this part. She never used to be like this. She used to be comfortable with her entire body. She'd never had an issue being naked in front of anyone.

"If you don't do it, I will," he warned.

She took a huge breath, blew it out. It was like a bandage, she rationalized. The faster you ripped it off, the less it stung.

With one quick jerk, she shoved her panties down and kicked them off.

"All right then, let's see it." He made a spinning gesture with his finger. "Turn around."

He wanted to look at it?

She felt like a bug under a microscope. A really big microscope. "Do you have to?"

"'Fraid so. Round you go."

"Okay, but I warned you." She tightened her muscles, desperate to make herself look a little smaller, and turned with her back to him. She waited for the gasp of horror, but he was silent. For the longest time he didn't make a sound, until she began to feel more annoyed than embarrassed.

"Hello, anyone back there?" She looked over her shoulder at him.

He was smiling. "Just enjoying the view."

She'd been with her share of men, probably too many for her own good, but Liam stood in a class all by himself.

"Well?" she asked.

"Perfect, just as I expected."

"Uh-huh."

"I can prove it."

"Sure you can."

He slipped his arms around her, flattening his hands over her stomach, and pulled her to him. She gasped as their bodies touched, his chest and thighs cupping her, molding her to him in a perfect, seamless fit.

"See," he said, his voice husky. "Perfect."

He was right. It *was* perfect.

He kissed her shoulder, her neck, cupped her breasts in his hands. She stopped worrying and concentrated instead on how good it felt nestled up to him.

He turned her around and drew her against him. Another perfect fit. He gazed down into her eyes. His were dark with desire, heavy with lust.

The most amazing thing was, they were standing there naked, touching each other just about as intimately as two people could, and they hadn't even kissed yet.

Not a real kiss.

It would be a shame, she thought wryly, if they had come this far only to find that they were totally incompatible when it came to kissing. But deep down she knew that wasn't possible.

As if reading her mind, he lowered his head. Her eyes slipped closed an instant before his lips brushed across hers. Sweet at first, tender, as though they both wanted to draw this out, make it last. He kissed as gracefully as his body moved, as passionately as he danced. His mouth tasted as rich and sweet as her favorite dessert.

It was almost eerie, how well they seemed to know each other. He eased her down onto the bed, and they lay next to each other, touching and exploring. More than once she caught herself wondering if this was a dream. If she would suddenly wake up in her bed back home to find none of this had happened.

Nothing real could be this good. And when he finally claimed her, sank inside her, slow and deep, for the first time in her life she felt complete. She knew that this was what making love was all about.

She peaked and shattered in his arms, knowing in her soul that this was how it was supposed to feel. He was a part of her now, as familiar as her own reflection.

And in four days she had to let him go.

SEARCHING THE STATEROOM HAD been a waste of time.

Claire was wearing the pendant. Tracy had seen her grasping it when she walked into the auditorium.

If only she had made her move the other night. Claire had been so blitzed she probably wouldn't haven't noticed it was missing.

Yet another mistake Tracy would have to learn to live with.

The original plan had been to search the room, put everything back exactly as she had found it, and sneak away without leaving a trace. But the longer she'd looked, the angrier she'd become. She kept thinking of Franco and how much he must miss her, and all the dumb mistakes she had made, and soon she was throwing things around the room, taking out all of her pain and frustration.

She was just lucky that no one had heard and caught her.

She felt guilty enough for what she had done, but when she saw the light fixture flying down toward Mr. Miles, her heart had stopped. He could have been killed. Lily, too. And maybe even Tracy herself if she had been standing too close. Whatever was going on, it was getting way out of hand.

As she left the auditorium and walked to the elevator, she couldn't help wondering if Salvatore might be to blame for all these disasters. Could he be on the ship?

But that didn't make sense. What good would disrupting the show do him? If nothing else, it was making things worse. With security on high alert, she wasn't sure how she would get the pendant now.

She pressed the button for the elevator and waited.

She had dance practice in twenty minutes, when all she felt like doing was curling up in bed and crying. She wanted her son back. She wanted to hold him and stroke his hair, assure him that everything would be okay and she would never let him go again.

Every time she thought things were at their worst, that the ache couldn't be more intense, she was proved wrong.

But she had to keep going. She had to be strong for Franco. If he lost her, who would be left? A father who could barely stand the sight of him, who would probably raise him to be a criminal?

The elevator opened and she stepped inside. Just before the doors shut a man stepped on with her. He wore an expensive looking silk shirt and a cap that shaded his face. But something about him was familiar.

Then he looked at her and her blood ran cold.

She found herself face to face with Kirk Rimstead, Salvatore's sleazy business partner.

How had he gotten on the ship?

"Surprised to see me?" he asked, flashing her a leering grin.

She felt sick to her stomach. "What are you doing here?"

"Sal's not happy with your lack of progress. He sent me to do your job for you."

"It was you that attacked Claire Mackenzie, wasn't it?"

He only smiled.

This was bad. Tracy needed the pendant, but she

didn't want to see anyone hurt. Rimstead was ruthless. He would stop at nothing to get the pendant from Claire, even if that meant killing her.

She summoned every bit of courage she could dredge up. "You wasted your time. I'm going to get it."

"It's too late for that. Sal is tired of waiting. We both are. By tomorrow night I'll be off the ship with the pendant in my hand."

That pendant was her only hope, her only bargaining chip. "What about Franco?"

"That's between you and Sal. But if I know him, he will say a deal is a deal. And you didn't hold up your end of the bargain."

Trey felt as though the floor had dropped out from under her. This could not be happening. Everything she loved, everything she had worked so hard for was slipping from her grasp.

Her only choice, only hope, was to get to the pendant first.

"By the way, Sal asked me to give you a message."

It happened so fast, she didn't have time to defend herself, not that she had much of a chance against a man like him. His arm flew out and he backhanded her hard against the right side of her head. Pain exploded through her skull and rattled her teeth. As she went down, she vaguely registered the sting of her ankle twisting.

Dazed, her head throbbing, she looked up to see the elevator door closing. Rimstead was gone.

"I REALLY HAVE TO GET back to work," Liam told Claire. And like the last three times he'd said it, she looped her arms around his neck, trapping him against the warm softness of her body.

She rubbed herself against him. "Not yet."

He felt his body stir, his pulse shift. He really did have to go.

She kissed his throat, his chin, the corner of his mouth. "Five more minutes."

The woman was insatiable.

"That's what you said thirty minutes ago." He had been here too long already. Long enough to raise suspicions. "You told your grandfather you would meet him for supper and it's nearly half past six."

Mr. Miles had called more than an hour ago to "check" on Claire and ask if it was all right that he stay with Lily for a while. Liam didn't doubt for a minute that he knew exactly what Liam and Claire were up to, and thankfully the idea didn't seem to offend him. He might not be so tolerant if he knew how very temporary this arrangement would be.

"I really do have to go."

Claire sighed, kissed him one last time, then let her arms fall from around his neck. He rolled out of bed and grabbed his clothes from the floor. They were a wrinkled, rumpled mess.

Why not pin a note to his back that announced *Recently Shagged?*

He would have to stop at his quarters and change.

Claire sat up, knees tucked under her chin, watching

him dress. He liked her this way, all disheveled and sexy, her skin flushed. Yet he also had an undeniable fondness for her coy, apprehensive side.

"When will I see you again?" she asked.

He shoved his legs into his trousers and fastened them, then pulled his shirt over his head and tucked it in. "I have to work tonight. But I could probably sneak away around ten."

"And sneak to my room?"

Absolutely. "How can I resist an offer like that?"

It was a risk, someone might see, but it was one he was willing to take. As far as he was concerned, ten o'clock couldn't come soon enough.

"You'll be working at the club, right?"

"Right." He spotted his I.D. badge on the floor and clipped it to his shirt. His radio was half under the bed. He attached that to his belt and switched it back on.

"If I come there, would you dance with me?"

He would dance with only her if his job description allowed it.

"Of course." He leaned over and kissed her. "You won't be jealous, seeing me dance with all those other women?"

"It's just work, right?"

"That's right."

This was going to be complicated. Someone was going to end up hurt, maybe both of them. But right now, he couldn't help thinking it would be worth it.

THE ENTIRE CAST ASSEMBLED for dinner that night in the Garden Terrace buffet.

During the salad, Eleanor leaned close to Claire. "Did you hear what happened to Tracy?" she said in that conspiratorial, just-between-us tone, but loud enough for the entire table, and probably half the dining room, to hear.

Claire didn't doubt that she was trying to stir up trouble again.

"She twisted her ankle and fell. I hear she banged her head up pretty good on the way down. A couple of passengers found her in the elevator half-conscious and helped her to the infirmary."

"Is she okay?" Claire asked.

"I guess she will be, but she won't be able to perform in the chorus line opening night."

Everyone at the table exchanged identical looks of apprehension. No one said it, but Claire knew exactly what they were thinking.

Claire reached up and touched the pendant.

"Of course, after what happened today," Eleanor added, "there may not be a show."

"Do they know why the lights fell?" one of the other women asked Papaw.

Eleanor didn't give him a chance to answer. "*I* heard that not too long ago people were using the ship to transport stolen antiquities. And ever since then, strange things have been happening. Maybe one of the thieves is still on the ship."

"What would an antiquities thief want with a bunch of old-timers?" Papaw said.

"They're going to ask us tomorrow what we want to do," Lily said. "If we want to keep going or quit."

"We've come this far," one of the men said. "I'm not quitting now."

"Me neither," the woman beside him piped in. "Whoever is doing this, we can't let him get the best of us."

Heads nodded in agreement.

"Even if it means dying?" Eleanor asked.

Claire sat there silently, torn between supporting the cast and Liam, and concern for everyone's safety. Liam told her that security was working every possible angle, and that they would solve the mystery, but she was tired of sitting around doing nothing.

She glanced at her watch. She had planned to meet Liam in the club, but wouldn't it be better to get to the bottom of this once and for all?

Maybe she could follow members of the cast around, see if she noticed anyone suspicious looking. It was a long shot, but she had to do something.

WITHIN AN HOUR CLAIRE realized what a stupid idea this spying thing was. She didn't have the chutzpah to sneak around and hide in dark corners, doing surveillance. She was so riddled with guilt, she couldn't shake the eerie sensation that someone was following *her*. Watching her watch them.

She was making herself paranoid.

Her career as a P.I. ended before it began, and to top it all off, she'd wasted an entire evening she could have spent near Liam. By the time she made it to the club, he wasn't there.

She circled twice, and asked a few of the dancers she recognized if they had seen him, but they all said he'd left a while ago. So where could he be?

She tried the obvious places first. The auditorium, the deck where they'd gone once before. But it was as if he'd vanished.

Realizing finally that it was hopeless, and feeling like a complete idiot, she gave up and went back to her room. She held out the hope that when she stepped off the elevator on her deck, he would be standing outside the door waiting for her. But the hallway was empty.

Maybe he'd left her a phone message, she thought as she opened the door. The lights were on, which was weird, because she could swear she'd shut them off before she left for dinner.

And the message light on the phone wasn't flashing. Damn.

She shut the door and tossed her purse on the love seat, unsure of what to do next. Then she heard a noise and froze. Could Papaw have stopped by? But why would he?

She heard the sound again and realized it was coming from the bathroom. She spun around just as the bathroom door opened.

It wasn't Papaw, and she definitely wasn't alone.

CHAPTER SEVENTEEN

"YOU SCARED ME half to death!" Claire said, slapping a hand over her heart to keep it from bursting through her chest.

Liam stood in the bathroom doorway, rubbing his hair dry with a towel, a second towel wrapped loosely around his hips. "Didn't mean to give you a fright."

And oh, my, did he look yummy.

The heady rush of arousal was instantaneous and intense. It had been an awfully long time since she had been this attracted to a man.

He hung the extra towel on the doorknob and raked his hair back with his fingers. The lean muscle in his arms and shoulders rippled under faintly freckled skin. Each little flex made her heart jump. "You're probably wondering what I'm doing here, and how I got in."

A little, but she was more interested in seeing what was under the towel. "How did you?"

"A key."

"You stole a key to my room?"

"It was given to me. By Lily, who got it from your grandfather."

"Seriously?"

"I was a bit surprised myself."

"I was looking all over for you. When did you see Lily?"

"While *I* was looking for *you*. You didn't come to the club. I figured this is where you would eventually end up, so when Lily gave me the key, I came to wait for you. I hope you don't mind that I borrowed your shower. My roommate was using ours and I didn't want to come by too late."

She so did not mind. He could use her shower any time.

"Sorry I was a no-show at the club." She pulled her shirt over her head and stepped out of her skirt. "But we can talk about that later."

He watched her bra slip away and her panties drop to the carpet. "Why later?"

She slipped her fingers under the edge of the towel, brushing his taut, warm stomach, and tugged it loose.

"Because right now," she said, as it dropped to his feet, "we have more important things to do."

"So YOU THOUGHT YOU could find a suspect?" Liam asked, feeding Claire another cookie from the welcome basket. They lay naked, stretched out in bed together, and though it was nearly one a.m., he wasn't the least bit tired. Good thing, because nothing he did seemed to wear her down, to slake her insatiable sexual appetite.

He could get used to this.

"I figured it was worth a try," she said, feeding him a gourmet chocolate.

"And your conclusion?"

"I'm not P.I. material."

Liam stroked her shoulder, the curve of her breast. He couldn't seem to make himself stop touching her.

"Is it true about Tracy?" Claire asked. "That she was hurt?"

"Word travels fast. She took a spill and banged her head."

Claire sat up, looking concerned. "Is she okay?"

"She wrenched her ankle and wound up with a mild concussion. She should be all right in a day or two, but she won't be performing in the chorus of the show."

"Some of the cast think it happened *because* of the show."

"Tracy herself said it was a fall. What reason would she have to lie?"

"Maybe the cast could chip in and order flowers for her."

"I'm sure she would like that."

"There's one chocolate-covered cherry left," she said. "You want to split it?"

She held it up to his mouth and he bit off half. The sugary filling oozed out, dripping down his chin and onto his chest.

"Oops! Let me get that." She used her tongue to lap up the sticky syrup, long slow licks. Purrs of pleasure curled in her throat as she worked her way down…

He wasn't ready to settle, he reminded himself as she licked her way down his stomach.

He liked his life simple.

But as she sank lower and took him in her mouth, he couldn't bloody well remember why.

THE CAST VOTED unanimously to keep the show going.

With so little time left together—was it really only two days?—Claire had hoped to spend the following evening alone with Liam. Unfortunately, he had a mile-long list of things he needed to do to prepare for the dress rehearsal tomorrow evening and the actual show the night after. And the only way to see him, to be close to him, was to volunteer her time. Which she happily did. She helped organize costumes and props. Put last minute touches of paint on the set pieces.

A new backdrop had been delivered, and though it wasn't as dramatic as the first, it would add a touch of elegance.

She and Liam hadn't gotten a heck of a lot of sleep the night before, and around eleven she started yawning. By midnight her eyelids were drooping, and at twelve forty-five she collapsed into one of the theater seats to rest her eyes for a few minutes.

The next thing she knew, Liam was nudging her shoulder. "Wake up, Sleeping Beauty."

She felt drugged with exhaustion. She pried her eyes open and looked up at him. "Hey, aren't you supposed to kiss Sleeping Beauty to wake her?"

Through fuzzy vision she saw him smile.

He crouched down beside her seat. "It would be my pleasure, but the dwarves are watching."

"That's Snow White, genius." She glanced up at the stage. There were only a few people left that she could see. "What time is it?"

"Almost two. Why don't you head up to your room? Get some rest."

She would be all alone. Normally that wouldn't have bothered her. She lived alone, slept alone every night. For the longest time she'd preferred it that way.

Now, for some reason, the idea held no appeal at all. "What about you?"

"The way things are going, I may have to pull an all-nighter. They're having trouble with the sound board and I need to be here to see that the problem's taken care of. It seems as though anything that could go wrong with the show has."

"Don't tempt fate. Things can always be worse."

"You're probably right."

"Here, you need this more than I do." She lifted the pendant from around her neck. She felt almost naked without its weight resting there. "Maybe it will bring you good luck, too."

"I couldn't."

"Take it." She was pretty sure she'd gotten everything from it that she could. The only thing she could possibly want now, the only thing left, was completely out of her grasp. All the good luck in the world wouldn't change that. "I know it's kind of bulky, but you can hide it under your shirt."

"Thank you." He leaned over and let her slip it over his head. "I'll wear it with pride."

He rose to his feet, pulling her up with him. "It's late. I'd better walk you to your room." He called to one of the men on the stage. "I'm walking Ms. Mackenzie to her room. I'll be back shortly."

At least they might get a little time together.

He touched her elbow, leading her up the aisle and out the door. She wished they could hold hands. They did that a lot when they were alone. As though they were taking advantage of every second that they could steal. She would always remember that for this short period in time she'd had everything she could possibly hope for. She was happy.

They were both quiet on the elevator and the walk to her door. Maybe Liam was also thinking about how little time they had left.

He unlocked the door and pushed it open. The room was dark and quiet and uninviting.

Lonely.

"I'll see you tomorrow," he said.

"When?"

"Probably early. We have dress rehearsal."

"When will you sleep?"

He shrugged. "After the show, I suppose."

"All in a day's work, huh?"

"The truth is, I'm going to be relieved when this is over."

"The show will be awesome. I know it will." She gestured inside. "Can you come in for a minute?"

"I shouldn't. I have to get back."

"Just one little minute," she coaxed.

He grinned, leaning against the door frame. "Your perception of time differs slightly from the average person's. You say five minutes when what you really mean is thirty."

"But if you don't come in, I can't kiss you goodnight." She looked up at him with her gooey eyes. "It will only be one minute. I promise."

He glanced up and down the hall. "Okay, but only *one.*"

She backed inside. He checked the hallway one last time and followed her in, shutting the door behind them.

"One minute," he repeated, then lowered his head to kiss her.

Their lips had barely brushed when the light switched on and a voice said, "I've been waiting for you."

CHAPTER EIGHTEEN

CLAIRE AND LIAM BOTH spun around in surprise. A man Claire had never seen before sat on her bed, helping himself to the last of the cookies in the welcome basket.

On second thought, he did look familiar. She had seen him in one of the bars last night, when she was spying on the cast, and he'd been sitting near them at dinner. But so many of the passengers' faces had become familiar that she'd thought nothing of it.

She hadn't been imagining someone was following her.

The satisfaction of knowing she was right lost its punch when she noticed the deadly looking knife lying on the bed beside him.

Liam saw it the same instant as Claire and stepped in front of her.

A voice in her head screamed at her to run, but before she could take a step, the man picked the knife up and pointed it at them. "I'd almost given up on you."

She gripped the back of Liam's shirt. She knew that voice. The unusual accent. She'd heard it before. But where?

Then it clicked. The arboretum.

He was the man who had mugged her.

Everything had been connected? The mugging? The show?

She needed to tell Liam, to let him know, but she was too stunned to do more than stand there and gape.

"What do you want?" Liam asked, sounding amazingly calm. How could he not be freaking out? The guy had a *knife*.

The man looked at Liam and smiled. A cold, evil grin that froze her pounding heart. "You have something I need."

"He's the one," she finally managed to say. "The one who mugged me."

"How kind of you to remember me."

"Who are you?" Liam asked.

She wondered how he could sound so composed. So...normal. She was shaking from the inside out.

The man walked slowly toward them. "I could tell you, but then I would have to kill you. Of course, I'm planning to kill you anyway." He gestured with the knife. "Away from the door."

Keeping Claire tucked behind him, Liam eased away, along the wall. "You can't kill us both at the same time. You don't think someone will hear?"

He nodded toward the sliding glass door. "You're about to have an unfortunate accident on the balcony."

At first she was confused, then she realized what he meant. *He was going to toss them over!*

It was a straight shot down to the water, but it was a

long way down. Even if someone were to see them fall and call for help, Claire doubted they would survive the impact.

They were almost at the sliding glass door, less than a yard away from the knife. They had to do something. Then she realized Liam was using the hand behind his back to work the knobs on his radio. Was he calling for help?

It squawked suddenly, startling both her and the mugger.

Claire saw a quick flash of movement, and the next thing she knew, she was flying backward. Everything happened so fast that afterward, when security questioned her, she had a tough time relaying the exact chain of events. All she registered as she hit the floor was the sound of glass shattering. She instinctively curled into a ball, waiting for the pain, for the knife to tear through her.

When it didn't, her first thought was simply *Liam*.

Forgetting her fear, she shoved herself up, not even sure what it was she planned to do.

The man lay sprawled on the floor, dazed. Liam stood over him, the knife in his hand, and there was shattered safety glass everywhere.

When Liam saw her move, he looked over. "Are you all right?"

"Yeah, but…" She moved in his direction.

"Stay back." With his free hand he grabbed his radio, which had probably saved both of their lives, and called for security. "Did I hurt you?"

"Hurt me?" He'd *saved* her.

"When I knocked you down. Did I hurt you?"

She shook her head, and realized suddenly that *he* could be hurt. He could be bleeding internally or something.

Fear took such a strong hold on her she went numb with it. "Did he… Are you hurt?"

"He hit the balcony door. I'm fine."

Oh, thank God. If Liam had been hurt protecting her she would never forgive herself.

Protecting her.

That was exactly what he'd done.

The instant he saw the knife he'd stepped in front of her, and he'd kept himself there like a shield. He would have traded his own life for hers without batting an eyelash.

"What happened?" she asked. "I heard the radio, then…"

"I kicked him."

"You *kicked* him?"

On the floor, the man groaned and cradled his arm. It was twisted grotesquely, the bone jutting out from the skin.

"I kicked the knife out of his hand and he fell into the glass."

That must have been one hell of a kick.

"Go open the door," Liam said. "Security should be here any second."

On unsteady legs she wobbled over to the door. It was starting to hit her now. That rush of adrenaline. The detached, surreal sensation that this could not possibly be happening to her. That she was standing on the outside looking in at someone else's life.

With a trembling hand she pulled the door open, screeching with alarm to find herself staring down the barrel of a gun. In the instant it took her to register that the person on the opposite end was a member of the ship's security staff, she'd lost a good ten years off her life.

"In here," Liam called, and the room was suddenly flooded with men in uniforms.

And all Claire could think, as they led her away, was that Liam wasn't supposed to be in her room, and he was going to get fired.

IF SOMEONE HAD ASKED Claire a week ago, she would have sworn up and down that her days of lying to the authorities were over.

Of course, what she told Sean wasn't exactly a lie. Liam *had* walked her to her room, and when she'd opened the door they'd seen the man sitting there. She simply neglected to mention the part about her and Liam preparing to play tonsil tag. Or the fact that they were in the room with the door closed when the lights came on.

A few more days of this, and she would know the ship's security office as well as the L.A. police station.

At least one thing was clear. They had caught the saboteur. The show and everyone working on it were finally safe.

Papaw and Lily were waiting when Sean finished questioning her. Thankfully someone had brought them up to date, so she didn't have to rehash what had happened for the millionth time.

"Sweetheart," Papaw said, drawing her into his arms and holding her.

Lily patted her shoulder. "You look exhausted."

She'd passed "exhausted" at three-thirty.

"We've already moved your things into Lily's room," Papaw said. "Lily and I can stay in my room."

"I'd really rather not be alone."

"I'll stay with you in your room, Claire," Lily offered. "I'm sure they could bring a roll away for you."

With Papaw on one side of her, and Lily on the other, they walked to the elevator.

"Have you talked to Liam?" she asked. Security had questioned them separately, and that had been a few hours ago.

"He's still in the security office," Lily said. "But he knows where you'll be."

"Do they know who the man is?"

"Liam told me that he had no identification and he isn't talking. The Mexican authorities will take custody when we dock in the morning."

"But he's the one responsible for everything that's happened?"

"That's what they believe."

"But they don't know?"

"Sweetheart," Papaw said gently. "Who else could he be?"

She wanted proof. She needed to know for sure that he was the one. That everyone was safe.

When they got to Lily's room, the first thing Claire did was take a long hot shower. When she stepped out of the bathroom the lights were out. Lily was already asleep and the roll away was set up beside the love seat.

Claire crawled under the covers, her hair still wet, and instantly sank into a deep dreamless sleep. She roused when Lily left for breakfast with Papaw a few hours later, then fell back to sleep and had strange dreams. It was nearly noon when a knock at the door drove her out of bed. She stumbled to the door, still half asleep, and pulled it open.

It was Liam. "Good morning. Or should I say good afternoon?"

She probably looked horrible, her hair a matted mess, but she grabbed his arm and pulled him inside. When the door was closed, she threw herself into his arms.

He wrapped her up tight and for a while they just held each other. It was hard to fathom how close they had come to dying. He'd risked his life for her.

He stroked her hair, her back. "Are you okay?"

"I am now." She rubbed her face against his shirt, breathed in his scent. There was no doubt about it, he was the one. "Did you get any sleep?"

"A little."

She looked up at him. His eyes were tired.

"Everything should be ready for dress rehearsal this afternoon."

"And the saboteur is in custody."

"The Mexican authorities took him away this morning."

She nuzzled against him again. She could never be close enough. "And you think he's the right one?"

"I have no reason to believe he isn't."

There was another knock at the door, startling them both.

"I guess we're still a bit jumpy," Liam said.

Claire looked out the peephole. Oh, crap. "It's Patti. Did she follow you?"

He shrugged. "I don't think so."

"Yes!" Claire called through the closed door.

"It's Patti, Ms. Mackenzie. Could I speak with you?"

"Just a minute," she called, then ordered Liam, "Hide."

Mumbling under his breath, he stepped into the bathroom and closed the door. Claire finger-combed her hair, opened the door and peeked out. "Yes?"

"Do you have a minute?"

"I'm not dressed. Is something wrong?"

"No, I just wanted to talk to you about what happened last night."

Again? "I already spoke to security."

"I came to apologize, for all the trouble. And to give you this." She handed Claire an envelope. "It's two vouchers for a free cruise. Our way of saying thank you for being so understanding."

In other words, thanks for not suing us, Claire thought. But she couldn't really blame the cruise line.

They did what they could to keep everyone safe. She took the envelope. "I look forward to coming back."

"If there's anything we can do, anything at all, please don't hesitate to ask. We should have a room ready for you by this evening."

Claire would ask if Liam could have the next two days off, but that might be a little too obvious. "There is one other thing. You should give Liam a big bonus for saving my life. If he hadn't been there, I would probably be shark bait."

It still made her shiver to think how close they had both come to being killed.

Patti smiled. "His efforts will not go unrewarded. I give you my word."

"In that case, I'd really like to get back to sleep." Lie, lie, lie.

"I won't keep you. Call if you need anything."

She turned to leave and Claire closed the door.

Liam was standing in the bathroom doorway grinning. "A bonus?"

"You deserve one. You saved my life. You disarmed a knife wielding maniac who planned to kill us. You should get a medal or something."

He shrugged. "Lucky shot."

"I was freaking out and you were so calm. It was like you did that kind of thing every day."

The amusement slipped from his face. "*Calm?* You think I was calm?"

Whoa.

The look on his face was dead serious.

"The thought of him hurting you…" He shook his head, as if he couldn't say the rest. Then he pulled her into his arms. He squeezed her so tight she could barely breathe. "I wasn't calm. I was scared half to death."

She burrowed against his chest, clung to him. "I love you, Liam."

The arms around her tightened, but he didn't say a word. Not that she'd expected him to.

"Claire, I…"

"You don't have to say anything. I just wanted you to know." How was it possible that after tomorrow she would never see him again?

"Claire, maybe we—" Liam's radio squawked and a scratchy, disembodied voice said, "Liam, come in."

She could feel the tension take hold of his shoulders and back. "What the bloody hell do they want now?" he mumbled, pulling the radio from his belt. She let her cheek rest against his chest. His heart was pounding like crazy. "This is Liam."

"We need you in the auditorium, pronto." It sounded like one of the stage hands.

"Can this wait? I'm a little busy."

"The saboteur was caught."

"No bleeding kidding," he snapped. "I was there."

"Not that one. The other one," he said.

Claire's head shot up.

"There was no other one?" Liam asked.

"There is now. A man was just caught tampering with the rigging, cutting through the rope."

Another saboteur?

She knew it. Deep down she had known there was someone else. Maybe that second sense Liam had had rubbed off on her.

"I'll be right there." He clipped the radio back on his belt and shook his head. "Bloody unbelievable."

Not to her it wasn't. "Give me two minutes to get dressed. I'm coming with you."

CHAPTER NINETEEN

"This is the other guy?" Claire said, when Liam handed her the copy of his passport photo. "Oh, my gosh, I must have seen him a hundred times around the ship. He's old."

"His name is Clint Chapman." Liam passed the photo to Lily and Frederick. "I take it the name sounds familiar?"

"I never would have recognized him," Lily said. "It's been so long."

Claire looked back and forth between them. "Who the heck is Clint Chapman? And why am I the only one who doesn't seem to know?"

"Clint Chapman is an actor," Lily said. "At least, he used to be."

"And he was a communist," Liam said. "And more than half the cast testified against him."

Claire's eyes widened and she turned to her grandfather. "Did you testify?"

"It was testify or be ruined. I didn't have a choice. And I told the truth."

"Chapman was here for revenge. He confessed to the

sabotage attempts. He swears he acted alone, but it's highly unlikely considering his age. Police are sure the other man is his partner. Chapman's already been transferred to the authorities. He could be charged as an international terrorist."

"I hope not," Lily said. "He's just a bitter old man who made some bad choices."

"I understand how they did it at first," Claire said. "But what about when the guards were there? How did they get in?"

"Chapman entered the auditorium posing as one of the cast, then hid in the prop room until everyone was gone. Because of his age, and the fact that he'd been coming and going since the first day of rehearsal, no one on the staff questioned it."

"But it's over," Claire said.

Liam nodded. "It's definitely over."

Frederick and Lily exchanged a look, and Liam had the distinct feeling there was something they weren't saying.

"Is anything wrong?" he asked.

"No, but there is something we need say," Frederick told them. Lily looked over at him and he nodded. "Go ahead."

Lily turned to Liam and Claire. She took a deep breath. "I'm not sure how to say this, so I guess I'll just say it. Frederick has asked me to marry him, and I've said yes."

"That's bloody fantastic!" Liam hugged her and shook Frederick's hand. It looked as though his matchmaking efforts hadn't been such a bad thing after all. "Congratulations!"

"Wow." Claire looked stunned by the news. It hadn't occured to Liam until just then that maybe she wasn't so keen on the idea.

"I know it seems quick," Lily told her. "But we figure at our age, what's the point in waiting?"

"Where will you live?"

"We haven't quite figured that out yet," Frederick told her. "We're still in the early planning stages."

Lily's brow wrinkled with concern. "Are you upset?" she asked Claire. "The last thing I want is for you to be hurt."

Liam held his breath. He knew Lily. If she thought the marriage would drive a wedge in Claire and Frederick's relationship, she would call the whole thing off.

"I just…" Claire sighed, and then smiled. "I'm not upset at all." She gave Lily a hug, then one to her grandfather. "I know you'll be really happy together."

The auditorium door swung open and members of the cast began to filter in.

"I guess it's time," Liam said, checking his watch. This dress rehearsal needed to go off without a hitch. But he had the feeling, with everyone's minds put to rest, the hard part was over. The show would be a success.

"We should head to the dressing room," Lily told Frederick, tugging on his sleeve. "Give the kids a minute alone."

"I'll be back there in a minute," Liam said. When they were gone, he told Claire, "You are upset. Aren't you?"

"Not upset, exactly." She shook her head. "This is going to sound really lame. But I think I'm jealous."

"Because you think Lily will take your grand-mother's place? Or yours?"

"It's not that."

"What is it then?"

"Don't take this the wrong way, but I'm jealous because I want what they have."

Liam's heart collided with the wall of his chest.

"I never thought I would hear myself say this, but I don't want to be alone anymore."

"Claire…"

"You know, I keep trying to come up with a way to make this work. I'm ready, but you're not, and I understand that. I would never ask you to change."

"I've been offered a job," he said. "One I'm seriously considering taking. There's a performance school near my hometown looking for a director."

"You would be an administrator?"

"And a teacher. And I would have the chance to choreograph and produce. It's what I've always wanted to do."

"What about your job here?"

"It was a good experience, but I never planned on it being permanent. In fact, I've already talked with Patti. I'll leave the ship when we dock tomorrow."

She took a deep breath, then forced a smile. "You need to do what makes you happy."

Claire was what made him happy.

He could see them a year from now, still feeling this

incredible connection. For the first time in his life, he could imagine spending forever with someone and never getting bored.

But was he ready for that?

"We could visit—"

"No." She shook her head. "You said that I deserve better, and you were right. I want all or nothing."

And she was right, she did deserve it. "I have to work tonight."

She nodded. "I know. I'd like to hang around and help, if that's okay."

"Of course. And I've already told Patti that after the show tomorrow night I'm off duty. We'll have all night."

She smiled, but it was sad smile. "I'd like that."

He hated to see her unhappy, to know he was the cause of it.

"Now go get to work," she said. "The cast is waiting for you."

The cast, the show, it meant little if she wasn't there with him.

THE DRESS REHEARSAL WENT off without a hitch, and all of their hard work paid off. The performance the following night was an enormous success. They played to a packed house.

Claire sat in the front row and watched, bursting with pride. The cast looked regal in their tuxedos and ball gowns. Their voices rang out loud and clear and the dancing was magical. And though she was probably biased, in her opinion Papaw and Lily stole the show.

Liam looked dashing in his tux, and he must have had fifty people come up to him afterward to congratulate him on his success. And he deserved all of it.

He was going to take this job, and he was going to be a huge success. He might even move on to bigger and better things. He could become world renowned.

She would get to say, *I knew him when...*

And she would be okay, too. She'd gotten over the hump. She wasn't afraid anymore. She was ready to put herself back out there. She doubted she would ever meet anyone like Liam, but that didn't mean she wouldn't find someone who could make her happy.

She was through hiding.

The cast gathered in the champagne bar, La Belle Epoque, afterward for a celebratory toast, and though she and Liam were counting the minutes before they could be alone, they had to make a brief appearance.

Tracy was there, too, and Claire cringed when she saw her. She was barely limping, but the side of her face, from her chin to her eye, was bruised and swollen.

"Your grandfather and Lily were amazing!" she gushed, giving Claire a somewhat awkward hug. "They really stole the show."

"Papaw never would have been able to do it without you."

She shrugged. "I think they probably would have, but they were fun to work with. After they got over being so mad at each other," she added. "By the way, you look awesome!"

"It was my grandmother's." Claire gazed with pride

at her jewel encrusted gown, the one her grandmother had worn the night Papaw won his first Oscar. It was a perfect fit, and it even made her butt look smaller.

"You're not wearing the pendant."

Claire reached up and touched her neck. "Nope. I lent it to a friend for good luck."

"Who?"

"Someone who needed it more than I do."

"I could use some good luck," Tracy said, touching the tender area below her eye. "I can't believe how clumsy I was."

"How are you feeling?"

"Still sore. But better."

"I'm glad. Everyone was really worried about you."

"Claire!" Liam called to her from the door. He gestured that it was time to leave.

"Well, I have to go, it was great seeing you!"

"You, too," Tracy said. She looked like she wanted to say something else, but Claire didn't hang around long enough to find out what it was.

It felt as if she and Liam hadn't been alone together for ages. When she reached the door, he looked as anxious as she did to escape. He grabbed her hand and practically dragged her to the elevator.

It took a second to register that he was touching her. In front of everyone.

"*Liam.*" She tried to tug her hand free, but he wouldn't let go.

He looked down at her and grinned. "I don't care."

He'd taken the job, she realized. That was why he didn't care. He had already given notice.

You're not going to think about that, she told herself as they rode the elevator up to her deck. When they got to her room, she rifled through her purse for her key.

"That dress is amazing," Liam said. He stood behind her, nibbled on her neck, her shoulder. He rubbed up against her, right there in the hallway, and she was too aroused to care that at any moment someone could turn the corner and see them. It didn't matter any longer.

She almost wanted to be caught.

"If you don't open the door now, we're shagging right here," he warned her, sinking his teeth into her neck. She felt him sliding her zipper down and realized he was serious. He really would take her right there in the hallway.

She found the key and unlocked the door. She barely had time to shut it before her dress hit the floor.

He tugged his tie loose and shrugged out of his jacket. But it seemed to take forever to fumble out of the rest of their clothes. She'd barely gotten his pants unzipped and he had her off her feet. He took her right there where they stood, swift and deep, against the wall. She cried out, felt her body clench around him. Eventually they moved to the floor, then finally the bed. They made love like that half the night, frantic and reckless. And when they were completely exhausted, with not an ounce of energy left between them, they just held each other.

"I don't want to say goodbye," he told her.

Tears welled up in her eyes, but she forced them back. This had been the most amazing night in her life and she wouldn't ruin it with a teary, emotional scene. "So we won't."

He brushed her lips with his. One of those sweet, tender kisses that never failed to melt her insides. "I love you, Claire."

For pity's sake, was he *trying* to make her cry?

"Me, too," she whispered. It was all she could manage without bursting into tears.

She must have fallen asleep shortly after that. The next time she opened her eyes it was morning. The first thing she saw was the pendant lying on the bedside table, right where Liam had left it. And when she rolled over in bed to reach for him, he was already gone.

"Are you sure you're okay?" Papaw asked her.

He sat at the foot of her bed, ready to go, waiting while she packed the last of her toiletries into her carry-on. Her body was going through the motions, working on autopilot.

She nodded, even though she was anything but *okay*. And at the moment, she didn't think she would ever feel *okay* again.

Wasn't she the one who had said no goodbyes? She just hadn't grasped the reality of that concept until she'd woken up alone.

Even though she knew deep down that it was best

this way, it didn't hurt any less, didn't ease the shaft of pain piercing her heart.

She'd been dumped before. Too many times to count. But this was different. This time it hurt so bad she could barely breathe.

"Are you almost ready?" Papaw asked. "We have to catch the shuttle to the airport."

When they got there, he would fly home with Lily, and she would catch a flight to Canada alone. She hadn't been gone two weeks, but it felt like a million years.

Probably the sooner she got off the ship, the sooner she got back to her life, to a routine, the better she would feel.

The same old dull, boring life hidden away on her island.

She zipped her case and hiked it over her shoulder. "I'm ready."

The elevator was crowded with departing passengers, and they had to squeeze in. The ship's lobby was even worse. She was almost to the door when she remembered the pendant still suspended from her neck. She had put it on one last time.

"I have to run back for something," she told Papaw. "I'll meet you outside."

"Is something wrong?"

She held up the pendant. "I have to give it back."

"Hurry!"

She turned around and ran smack into Tracy.

"Whoa! Hi!" the dancer said. "I was hoping to catch you before you left. I wanted to say goodbye."

"Oh, goodbye. Thanks again for everything." Claire pulled the chain over her head. "Hey, do you know who I should give this to?"

"Um, probably Patti. I'll take it for you."

"Are you sure?"

She held out her hand. "It's no problem, really."

Claire held the necklace out to her, then drew back her hand at the last second. "On second thought, I think I'll do it."

"You might miss your shuttle."

Papaw would hold it for her. Besides, it would only be right to return it herself. "I want to thank Patti."

"I'll tell her," Tracy insisted.

"No, really. I'd like to do it, but thanks."

Tracy's hand fell to her side and she nodded. She looked almost hurt. "Okay. Have a good flight home."

Claire found Patti in her office.

"Ms. Mackenzie," the cruise director said with a smile.

"I wanted to say goodbye. And thanks."

"I would ask if you enjoyed your trip, but I'm not sure I'd like the answer."

"Well, it wasn't boring, that's for sure."

"I hope you'll use the coupons and sail with us again."

"I plan to." She held out the necklace. "I wanted to give this back."

Patti took it. "Did it bring you good luck?"

"I'm alive," she joked. "So I guess so."

"I was thinking more about matters of the heart.

Everyone else who wore the pendant found their true love."

Claire opened her mouth to answer, but discovered a lump in her throat the size of a small country. She refused to break down now. At least not until she was home. In Vancouver.

Alone.

She swallowed hard. "It didn't work out."

"I'm sorry to hear that. He left not fifteen minutes ago."

Claire realized she meant Liam. Did she think that telling Claire he was gone was going to make her feel better?

"You'd better go or you'll miss your shuttle."

Claire nodded. If she tried to talk now she would definitely start blubbering.

Forcing back the tears welling in her eyes, she sprinted for the door. Hold it together, damn it. Just a few more yards and you're home free.

Papaw was waiting for her near the shuttle stop.

Liam was standing next to him.

He wore faded jeans, a T-shirt and tennis shoes and an enormous duffel sat at his feet. Off to his new job. His new life. The one he would spend without her.

She forced her feet to move, but with every step she took, she felt less like weeping and more like punching him in the nose.

What right did he have to torture her this way? Why didn't he just leave? No goodbyes, just like they had agreed.

She stopped in front of them, really ticked off now. At least it beat that constant urge to break down.

"Well, Lily," Papaw said, taking her bag. "We had better get on board."

They were bailing on her. Thanks a lot, she thought wryly.

Claire looked up at Liam, torn between wanting to hug him, and looking for the most effective place to kick him. "We said no goodbyes."

He had the gall to smile at her. He was breaking her heart and he was actually happy about it? "You said no goodbyes. So we won't say goodbye."

Was this some cruel joke? Did he get off torturing her? "So why are you standing here?"

"I'm going to go with you."

What? So he could hang around for a few days, maybe a week, then say goodbye? She shook her head. "No."

"No?"

"I won't do this. I won't take a few more days, and then have to watch you leave again. I don't want that."

"What do you want?"

"You know what I want." Like it even mattered at this point.

"A week? A month?"

She shook her head.

"I didn't think so." He sighed. "Then how would you feel about forever?"

Forever? Was he joking?

She opened her mouth, but nothing came out.

"Too long?" he asked.

He was doing it again, hiding behind humor. "What about your job?"

He shrugged. "There will always be another job. But, Claire, you are definitely one of a kind."

"So you're not going to take the offer? Just like that?"

"Just like that."

"Instead you're going to come to Canada with me."

"Unless you'd rather I didn't."

This was completely nuts.

"What will you do?"

"I'm sure I'll find something."

"Liam, Saltspring Island has a population of ten thousand, and they have one very small community theater. Trust me when I say you won't find anything."

He folded his arms across his chest, regarding her as if she were a loony person. He was offering to drop everything for her, and she was giving him a hard time.

The truth is, she'd never felt more sane, more together in her entire life.

"Is that your way of saying you don't want me to come with you?" he asked.

"I don't want you to come with me," she said. Be brave, Claire. It's time to stop being afraid and take a chance. "I'm coming with you."

"You're coming to England?"

"Why not?"

"You have a life, Claire. A home."

"Where does it say that you're the only one who

gets to make the sacrifices? If it's okay with you, I would like to be the martyr for a little while."

He raised his brows. "Martyr? Claire, think about what you're saying."

"I know exactly what I'm saying. I want to move to England, damn it. I want to be impulsive and have fun. I want an adventure." She poked him in the chest. "I want *you*."

He wrapped an arm around her waist, pulled her to him and kissed her. "Are you for real?"

"Is that a yes?"

"England it is. We'll have a million details to figure out."

"Probably."

"You'll want to find a job."

She shrugged. "Plants grow everywhere. How hard could it be?"

"You're really sure about this?"

"Completely."

The shuttle driver beeped the horn.

"Looks like it's time to go." He picked up his duffel and hoisted it over his shoulder. "Are you ready?"

She was so ready. In fact, it felt as if she'd been ready her whole life. "I'm ready. Are you?"

He smiled and held out his hand.

And she took it.

EPILOGUE

TRACY HAD HOPED TO have one last chance at the pendant, but Ariana had taken it straight to the safe, where it would sit until the next set of passengers boarded.

She dreaded her call from Salvatore.

At least she'd bought herself some time. Or Liam had. With Rimstead behind bars, Sal still needed her.

She watched from the ramp as Liam took Claire's hand and they boarded the shuttle together. At least someone had gotten a happy ending.

She was happy for them, and at the same time she burned with jealousy. She needed to see Franco. Needed to know that he was okay.

And now all she could do was wait. But one thing was clear.

She had one last chance and she couldn't blow it.

* * * * *

MEDITERRANEAN NIGHTS

*Join the glamorous world of cruising with the guests
and crew of* Alexandra's Dream—*the newest luxury
ship to set sail on the romantic Mediterranean.*

The voyage continues in May 2008 with
THE WAY HE MOVES
by Marcia King-Gamble

Heiress Serena d'Andrea has trouble trusting
the men she meets, but while on a cruise aboard
Alexandra's Dream she finds a pendant that promises
to bring the wearer luck in love.
Yet, from the moment Serena puts it around
her neck, she's beset by mishaps.
Luckily Gilles Anderson is always around to come
to her rescue, and strangely, he looks uncannily
like Marc, a man from her past—a man she once
thought she could love.

Here's a preview!

THE CLUB WAS FILLED with a diverse group of people, ranging from officers to women on the prowl. Serena scanned the crowd hoping to find Marc already seated, but couldn't spot him. There wasn't a vacant table to be found so she approached the bar. She'd have a glass of red wine, wait a few minutes to see if he would show up, and then move on.

She was about to place her order when she felt a tap on her shoulder. Serena swung around and came face to face with the man she was looking for.

"There you are," Marc LeClair said, a mischievous twinkle in his eyes indicating he was pleased to see her. The cleft in his chin was even deeper than she remembered. He held a cup of dark liquid in his hand. "The hotel and cruise directors were here only a minute ago, and then they got paged and went rushing off somewhere. I thought you'd stood me up so I went to the Espresso Bar to drown my sorrows. Shall we try to find seats?"

"Stood up" implied they were on a date. He couldn't possibly be thinking of picking up where they had left off.

"There's no place to sit," she said, refusing to acknowledge her quickening pulse and the heightened awareness of the man standing beside her. Marc wore an open-necked shirt with the sleeves rolled up to reveal tanned, corded forearms. His dress slacks were immaculately pressed with a sharp crease to them, and his tasseled, leather loafers were shiny. He smelled like an exotic Asian spice. And just like she remembered.

"If I can get hold of a waiter I'll order us drinks and we can take them to the library," Marc suggested.

"I promised to buy you a drink," Serena reminded him.

"You can get the next one."

Ten minutes later they were seated on one of the library's leather couches, brandy snifters in hand.

"With the exception of that earlier unpleasant incident, are you enjoying yourself?" Marc asked when they'd settled in.

"Oh, yes. The show was wonderful, like being in Las Vegas, I'm told. The dancers were beautiful women and very talented."

"None as stunning as you. Have you been to Las Vegas?"

Serena smiled back at him. She was beginning to get a warm, tingly feeling all over, but she attributed it to the drink and not Marc.

"You're too kind," she said. "No, I've never been to Las Vegas. Have you?"

"Yes, on business."

"Tell me about it."

"It's a fun place to visit but I'm not sure I'd want to live there," he added. "And it's definitely not a place to raise kids."

"Do you have children?" Serena eyed him over the rim of her brandy snifter.

"Yes, one daughter." He didn't elaborate further.

The cognac was beginning to loosen her tongue.

"And where is this daughter of yours?"

"She lives with her mother."

Serena was going by pure intuition. But the more they spoke, the more she was convinced this was Marc. She'd spent enough time with him to note a couple of personal habits, like the way he outlined the cleft of his chin with one finger when he was thinking. Marc was doing exactly that right now.

She reached over and placed a hand on his arm. "Are you sure you have never visited my country?"

His dreamy blue eyes drifted over her. "I've forgotten which country that is."

"Argentina. Buenos Aires."

"And you ask because…?"

"You remind me of a man I was involved with."

"And if I were this man, why would I pretend not to know you?"

"Only you can answer that."

A couple came wandering into the library. They were holding hands and talking quietly.

They circled the room several times before taking a seat on an adjacent couch.

"We thought we'd have a quick aperitif before going

to the piano bar," the man said. "The pianist is awesome."

Marc took Serena's almost empty glass from her and set it down on the table. He stood and held out his hand.

"And we're on our way to the Polaris Lounge to listen to big band music. Maybe we'll even dance."

Serena accepted the hand he offered and stood. She hadn't been expecting an evening of dancing. But now she would know for sure whether Gilles Anderson and Marc Le Clair were one and the same.

Two different people would not have identical moves.

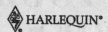
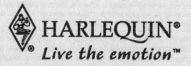

REQUEST YOUR FREE BOOKS!

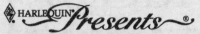

2 FREE NOVELS PLUS 2 FREE GIFTS!

YES! Please send me 2 FREE Harlequin Presents® novels and my 2 FREE gifts (gifts are worth about $10). After receiving them, if I don't wish to receive any more books, I can return the shipping statement marked "cancel". If I don't cancel, I will receive 6 brand-new novels every month and be billed just $4.05 per book in the U.S. or $4.74 per book in Canada, plus 25¢ shipping and handling per book and applicable taxes, if any*. That's a savings of close to 15% off the cover price! I understand that accepting the 2 free books and gifts places me under no obligation to buy anything. I can always return a shipment and cancel at any time. Even if I never buy another book, the two free books and gifts are mine to keep forever.

106 HDN ERRW 306 HDN ERRL

Name	(PLEASE PRINT)	
Address		Apt. #
City	State/Prov.	Zip/Postal Code

Signature (if under 18, a parent or guardian must sign)

Mail to the **Harlequin Reader Service:**
IN U.S.A.: P.O. Box 1867, Buffalo, NY 14240-1867
IN CANADA: P.O. Box 609, Fort Erie, Ontario L2A 5X3

Not valid to current subscribers of Harlequin Presents books.

Want to try two free books from another line?
Call 1-800-873-8635 or visit www.morefreebooks.com.

* Terms and prices subject to change without notice. N.Y. residents add applicable sales tax. Canadian residents will be charged applicable provincial taxes and GST. This offer is limited to one order per household. All orders subject to approval. Credit or debit balances in a customer's account(s) may be offset by any other outstanding balance owed by or to the customer. Please allow 4 to 6 weeks for delivery. Offer available while quantities last.

Your Privacy: Harlequin Books is committed to protecting your privacy. Our Privacy Policy is available online at www.eHarlequin.com or upon request from the Reader Service. From time to time we make our lists of customers available to reputable third parties who may have a product or service of interest to you. If you would prefer we not share your name and address, please check here. ☐

HP08

SPECIAL EDITION™

THE WILDER FAMILY
Healing Hearts in Walnut River

Social worker Isobel Suarez was proud to
work at Walnut River General Hospital, so
when Neil Kane showed up from the attorney
general's office to investigate insurance fraud,
she was up in arms. Until she melted in his
arms, and things got very tricky...

Look for

HER MR. RIGHT?
by
KAREN ROSE SMITH

Available May wherever books are sold.

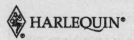

HARLEQUIN®

American ★ Romance®

Three Boys and a Baby

When Ella Garvey's eight-year-old twins and
their best friend, Dillon, discover an abandoned
baby girl, they fear she will be put in jail—
or worse! They decide to take matters into their
own hands and run away. Luckily the outlaws are
found quickly…and Ella finds a second chance
at love—with Dillon's dad, Jackson.

LOOK FOR

Three Boys and a Baby

BY

LAURA MARIE ALTOM

Available May
wherever you buy books.

LOVE, HOME & HAPPINESS

HARLEQUIN *Presents*

Don't forget Harlequin Presents EXTRA
now brings you a powerful new collection
every month featuring four books!

Be sure not to miss any of the titles in
In the Greek Tycoon's Bed,
available May 13:

THE GREEK'S
FORBIDDEN BRIDE
by Cathy Williams

THE GREEK TYCOON'S
UNEXPECTED WIFE
by Annie West

THE GREEK TYCOON'S
VIRGIN MISTRESS
by Chantelle Shaw

THE GIANNAKIS BRIDE
by Catherine Spencer